THE HISTORY OF SILENCE

THE HISTORY OF SILENCE

PEDRO ZARRALUKI

Translated from the Spanish by
Nick Caistor and Lorenza García

HB Hispabooks Publishing

Hispabooks Publishing, S. L.
Madrid, Spain
www.hispabooks.com

Originally published in Spain as *La historia del silencio* by Anagrama, 1994
First published in English by Hispabooks, 2014
English translation copyright © by Nick Caistor and Lorenza García
Design © simonpates - www.patesy.com

ISBN 978-84-942830-6-2 (trade paperback)
ISBN 978-84-942830-7-9 (ebook)
Legal Deposit: M-23612-2014

To Concha

Another took two loud sounds and out of them made a silence.
Another constructed a deep darkness out of two brilliant lights.

EDGAR ALLAN POE

We are all crazy about each other.

LUIS VÉLEZ DE GUEVARA

This is the story of how a book that should have been called *The History of Silence* never came to be written. Although common, failure is not easy to explain. There are remarkable people, capable of immense efforts, who manage to pull off what seems at first like the craziest of ventures. Unfortunately, we don't fall into that category. Just over two years ago, we embarked on research that was as thorough as it was chaotic. The findings could not have been more disappointing. The book you have in your hands is not the dissertation we had envisioned but rather the chronicle of a renunciation. The original idea had clearly been far too ambitious. Trying to discover what happens in those moments when nothing happens, trying to understand silence (and stillness, and darkness, and absence, and thought itself), even if only partially or subjectively, is so absurd an undertaking that even the most zealous enthusiasts (unfortunately, we are not in that category either) are doomed to fail. Our own efforts were exhausting, if not exhaustive, although on balance they probably weren't entirely without merit, if only because a few people believed in our idea and sent us a copious amount of information. A good example is our extremely talkative and outgoing dear friend Olga, who called one day to tell us that in the midst of a party in full swing she had remained two hours without moving a muscle or opening her mouth in silent, sincere tribute to our work. We thanked her enthusiastically, something we do really well. However, despite the heroic nature of her testimony, it opened up no new avenues for us to explore. By then, we had already spent endless hours considering the boundless potential of silence. For want of any better ideas, we had even tried not speaking to each other for a whole week, just to see whether we could stand being together without uttering a word. I was the one who broke our stupid pact in a moment of distraction, although Irene still imagines I did it in a fit of impatience. I had just come back from the supermarket and I emptied the shopping bags out on the kitchen table. Irene was already boiling water for the pasta in a pan. Then I gave her a heartbroken look (though she claims it was too casual for it not to have been somewhat deliberate) before announcing that I had forgotten the spaghetti. From that moment on, in our private language *I've forgotten the spaghetti* came to mean giving up on something out of a sense of overwhelming fatigue. And so, when Irene once managed to go four days without smoking, she said *I've forgotten the spaghetti* and lit a cigarette. And I said it while lying in bed, the moment I woke up, the day I decided to abandon my stubborn efforts to go to the gym every morning. And we both said it when we turned off the computer after spending an entire weekend trying to beat it at chess, and when we stopped eating only fruit on Thursdays, and whenever François came to give us French lessons in the evening and yet we decided to watch a film on TV instead. Since that fateful day when Irene and I started speaking to each other again, we regretted a hundred times over having forgotten the spaghetti, which leads me to believe that we spend our lives giving up on things, primarily those we are able to get only by our own efforts.

Irene and I reached a point where we overdosed on silence, although not long before it had seemed normal to us to be surrounded by sound. Not a single thought about the importance of sound or of its absence had ever crossed our minds. Our research into silence had its origins in an upheaval in our lives. Up until then Irene had worked as a freelance, making regular contributions to a publisher specializing in encyclopedias. She had just finished a series of installments, which, under the somewhat Hitlerian title *My One and Only Friend*, aimed at acquainting readers with the different breeds of dog. At that moment Irene was an authority on canines, just as, the year before, she had been a leading expert on experiments for young students. From the refraction index to Yorkshire terriers, each new project would make her forget all she knew about the previous one. Irene would boast that the way she amassed knowledge was very similar to the sex life of those who claim to be serial monogamists. What Irene could not have known was that the last canine entry would also mark the end of her association with the publisher. They called to tell her there was nothing new in the pipeline (which was untrue, because she knew they were compiling an encyclopedia on transportation as well as a series on lost civilizations), and advised her to look for another publisher, as they were about to carry out an imminent restructuring. In the world of freelance contributors, the term imminent restructuring means the publisher has decided to do without you. And so Irene was out of work, and that was just the start of our misfortunes. I had been writing a novel for the past three years, and to be brutally honest, the result was decidedly inferior to what I had when I began. At first impatient, and then worried, my publisher ended up looking at me with unremitting pity each time I announced (in an increasingly excited voice and an ever gloomier expression) the forthcoming conclusion of my book. What with one thing and another we were on the verge of financial collapse, if indeed the word collapse can be applied to something that has never had any substance, but has simply flowed like a river, or like life, or other elusive things. And so one morning, Irene and I found ourselves eating breakfast on our tiny terrace under the shade of the bamboo plants, and we realized we could go on eating breakfast forever because we had nothing better to do. After two hours engaging in that necessarily finite activity (how absurd to be still having breakfast as night fell), we decided to burn our boats and seize the opportunity to go on a trip. We rejected our initial ideas, splendid though they were, because of the cost. Then we considered more affordable destinations with less exotic names. I even pointed out, forgetting the person I was talking to, that neither the authors of great literature nor good travelers have ever needed costly settings. Irene remained serenely silent. She had always chosen *The Alexandria Quartet* over *Diary of a Country Priest*, with a vehemence that rejected the possibility that both novels might be excellent. For Irene, literature was a call from the far side of the mountain, and the main characters of all great novels had to be people who wandered off to remote places. As I was buttering my sixteenth slice of Melba toast, it struck me that Rioja was a place we had already enjoyed countless times through its wines. Our bodies had absorbed copious amounts of phosphorus, calcium and potassium from Rioja's soil. You could say we had drunk it down a thousand times without ever setting foot in the place. I suggested a trip there and Irene accepted enthusiastically.

"It'll be like a journey to the source of life," she said, a dreamy look in her eyes.

Two days later we were driving in a rented convertible across the Monegros Desert. It was June and already very hot. The sun was so fierce we didn't dare open the sunroof. Irene hummed as she saw the mileposts go by, and we felt quite happy. We drove down a long stretch of highway that seemed like the road to infinity. My hand nestled in Irene's lap. The purr of the engine lulled us. Suddenly, as if to wake us up, there was a ghastly screeching sound. Instinctively, I lifted my foot off the gas pedal, and when I pressed it down again we heard a noise like someone rattling a can full of nuts and bolts. The wheels hadn't locked, but nothing would get the car moving again. I pulled over to the side of the road. We opened the hood, because throughout history that is what people have always done when a car breaks down, regardless of whether they have any mechanical skills. We peered at the engine, from opposite sides of the vehicle. The contemplation of a car engine, which is invariably a heap of greasy, old machinery, offers few clues to the uninitiated. All I could do was sigh, at a loss as to how it had kept going until a few short moments ago.

"Maybe it's this tube here," said Irene, who was stubborn and headstrong, pointing randomly at a cylinder that looked frankly alarming.

One glance was enough to reveal several other parts that looked even more distressing. I climbed back into the car and turned the key in the ignition. But as soon as I pressed down on the accelerator the same rattle of nuts and bolts started up. I got out slowly, stretched my arms, and announced it was the transmission. I did so with the assurance of doctors when they diagnose a viral infection and tell you to give it time. And so we sat down on a rock and we waited. The air was still, the road deserted. Irene started humming again. The silence was so intense that her muffled voice seemed to emerge from everywhere at once. There were no trees around us, only a desolate landscape of fissured rocks. Then, very gradually, we became aware of a faint noise coming from somewhere. More precisely, we were suddenly aware that a distant noise had grown steadily louder until it became audible. We waited, and the sound grew louder. We could make out the shape of a car approaching on the road, but we did not move. It sped past us unleashing a tornado of sound, a sudden explosion that died away as slowly as it had announced its arrival. Moments later we found ourselves once again immersed in the same absolute calm. I closed my eyes, my head spinning slightly, and felt as if I was disengaging from the Earth. I found myself floating in the darkness of outer space, wallowing in infinite peace, in a relentless emptiness, where time and waiting didn't exist. My mind was a complete blank, and all I could feel was my own weightlessness. While I was daydreaming, a faint sound made me look to one side. And so I became an absent witness to the movement of our planet leaving in its wake a shimmering tail of light. The image passed me by just as the car had done, surrounded by a sudden tornado of banging, of noise and laughter. Then it spun away from me. As it disappeared into the darkness, peace returned, and at some point (impossible to say exactly when) I stopped hearing it completely and was enfolded by absolute calm.

I opened my eyes and looked at Irene. She too had closed her eyes. Her head was tilted back and her lips were quivering.

"We could write a book about silence," I said.

Her mouth curved into a smile, which broadened as her thoughts began to race. Irene's most dazzling smiles were the ones that came from deep inside. She remained motionless for a few more moments. Then she leapt to her feet and looked at me, brimming with enthusiasm.

"It will require an enormous amount of work," she said, tainted perhaps by an understandably (in her case) encyclopedic attitude. "Why did cinemas hire piano players during the silent movie era? Is silence bearable? Is there such a thing as silence or is it just an accumulation of distant sounds? Which do we find more nerve-racking: noise or the absence of noise? On the other hand, haven't we all at some point or another been forced to remain silent? Who did so out of self-interest, out of weakness or perversion? Who has saved and who condemned others by his or her silence? Can one spend a whole lifetime waiting for a question to be answered? Does absolute silence, the silence of God, really exist, or is it simply a metaphor for ignorance? Can silence be bottomless, as deep as a well? Can one feel comfortable inside a well? Why isn't absolute silence described as something boundless, like the calm, empty spaces of the universe? Can silence be methodical without seeming artificial? Have you ever been to a wake? Isn't it true that the only ones who behave naturally at a wake are the dear departed because they are so damned silent? On the other hand, is hearing nothing from a loved one for twenty years the most unbearable type of silence? Why do we wait patiently but not eternally for a simple word that would put an end to our pain? Why do we say that someone broke the silence instead of freeing the silence or calming it, which would be very poetic and would prevent that ringing in our ears we find so annoying? Why do we say someone is the silent type, as if they went through life on tiptoes, when in fact that person simply doesn't talk much? Is talking the most deliberate way to break the silence? Why does silence seem awkward at dinner parties and not on mountaintops? What happens at those rare dinner parties that are held on a mountaintop? How can keeping silent be the noblest and the most despicable act when what is being kept is exactly the same thing? Why don't you say something? You're letting me do all the talking. Is silence a betrayal of evolution, perhaps, and thus a fleeting omen that everything comes to an end?"

When Irene finally stopped talking, her agitated words lingered in the still air. I contemplated the barren landscape, thinking how difficult it was going to be to give shape to all this. But my mind was teeming with ideas. Irene and I looked straight at each other, both of us immersed in thought, that rigorously silent, overwhelming activity. I had the strange impression that everything around us had come to a halt, like the ominous calm that precedes the deadliest storms.

Irene and I had been together for five years, long enough for us to be unable to imagine life without the other, but not long enough for us to begin remembering the existence of other, all but forgotten, choices which were irrevocably drifting away. In short, we were going through the most stable, least anxiety-ridden stage of our relationship. The perfect moment to embark on a joint project. We lived in a cozy mezzanine apartment in Barcelona, much frequented by a wide variety of friends, ex-lovers, and friends of friends, who kept themselves entertained by inspecting our paintings and books, and smiled timidly. Irene loved seeing new faces in our living room. Within seconds she would already be merrily chatting with the newcomers, and every time she showed great interest in what they did, and always expressed genuine admiration for them. As it happened, we had such a wide circle of friends that we could only get around to seeing each one of them every three or four months (and only if we stretched our already bustling social life to the limit). As a result, I had refused to add a single new acquaintance to our endless list, and this made me keep my distance from the strangers who invaded our home. In fact, I adapted so easily to my state of semi-autism that I began to keep everyone at arm's length whether it was some unknown broody blonde gobbling up my meatballs, or an old friend from the Party who had come over eager to resume one of our heated debates. I gradually became the invisible man, except in reverse: I couldn't see them but they could see me. Irene found my ability to sit in my favorite armchair reading, while seven people around me plotted the takeover of the arts section of a daily newspaper, disconcerting and amusing in equal measure. After everyone had left and we climbed into bed, Irene would describe everything that had happened as if I hadn't been present. Outside our bedroom, the darkness of the apartment concealed the grime and chaos of much frequented places.

The mastermind behind all this disorder went by the name of Rosario. She was a small, garrulous woman (she was probably much younger than she looked). Every morning, Rosario arrived at eight o'clock, while we were still asleep, and began working in silence. It must have been excruciating for her to have to repress her natural ebullience. And so, the moment she saw us emerge in our bathrobes on a quest for coffee, she set about cheerfully compensating for all the noise she had choked back earlier. Rosario was an excellent energy booster in the mornings, but if we had time, Irene and

I used to take refuge on the terrace so as to eat our breakfast with a degree of calm. Rosario could make a stew, crowd the washing line with clean linen, mop every single inch of the apartment and fix a broken lamp simultaneously, without losing any of her cheerfulness. However, the most amazing thing about Rosario was her way of greeting people. If, for instance, I came home and Rosario was dusting the ceiling, she would turn around and her face would light up as if seeing me was the best thing that could have happened to her. Forgetting that greetings work at a distance, she would race down the ladder and caper toward me with dainty little steps. Then, only when we were face to face, would she begin waving her right arm as vigorously as if she were gesticulating to someone standing on the deck of a ship half lost in fog. And she did that to everybody. It made me extremely uncomfortable. All I could think of was how to slide past her, and I never could decide whether to go right or left. Irene, on the other hand, was perfectly content to mimic her. Seeing them standing face-to-face, giggling and waving at each other, one could swear they were cleaning the two sides of a window pane and taking immense pleasure in doing so. In any case, Irene clearly enjoyed sharing things with other people.

We never made it to Rioja, but we carried on drinking its wines. Arriving back in Barcelona was a little unsettling. We couldn't wait to begin our research, but we had no idea how to go about it. Irene, who was more methodical than me, decided to search for information at the Central Library and to talk to friends who worked in the fields of history, physics and philosophy.

She bought a huge blackboard, which she placed next to her desk. She spent the first few days creating files in her computer and drawing diagrams on the blackboard. I found all this fascinating, but was incapable of doing things in the same way as her. I wasted a ridiculous number of hours staring into space, before reaching the conclusion that I had to begin somewhere. I could start by stating the obvious, thus employing the same method that always worked well for me in my writing. I sat in front of a blank page and wrote a tentative beginning for our exhaustive work:

Silence, at least the type of silence discussed in this book, does not exist unless someone is there to consider it as such. That someone needn't be very substantial, but should at least have some sense of feeling. Silence was first broken (in the presence of a witness, and therefore with consequences, which is what interests us), shortly after the dawn of time, somewhere very far away in that place we now call Swaziland, in Southern Africa. The landscape there was decidedly hostile. The atmosphere, which contained very little oxygen, was convulsed by spectacular electrical storms. By then you could step on the ground (although there was no one to do so), although volcanoes were springing up everywhere. Their yawning craters spewed out vast amounts of magma. In spite of all this, in a warm-water pond, history's first tragedy was brewing. It is strange that the first little sound that interests us was almost inaudible (in fact, no human being would have been able to hear it) what with the hubbub that must have been going on everywhere at the time. It so happened that floating in the (swamp-like, putrid, noxious) pond was a sort of cellular membrane, a tiny sheet drifting all alone lost in the clamor of the elements. It was too primitive a creature for us to consider it cute. Yet it was the first living entity to reveal its existence by breaking the silence, and in geological terms this is not so different from the inexperienced burglar who knocks over a table in the dark. We cannot say for certain that it made a noise. Only that it was capable of tiny, spasmodic movements that allowed it to slide through the water. And it was just bad luck that the same pond was also inhabited by an amorphous, spongy creature, similar to a jellyfish, and much bigger than our tiny quivering sheet. The monster had no auditory system, but its gelatinous skin could feel the waves produced by the other creature's movements. In a fraction of a second, an ungainly tentacle grabbed hold of the cellular membrane and inserted it into a sinister orifice. One could hardly expect the two main characters of this tragedy, primitive beings that they were, to strike up a friendly conversation. We can therefore conclude that the first time a living creature became aware of another being in its immediate vicinity, it took the somewhat drastic decision to eat it, thus creating a cruel yet vital pathway toward the evolution of life on our planet.

"Thanks to you, I'll never be able to sleep as soundly as before," Irene reproached me a few days later. "I used to feel that sheets covered and protected me. Now I fall asleep worrying that I have to take care of them."

Once again I thought that Irene gave too much importance to what everyone else did, and also that she was completely out of her mind. Even so, that night, when I climbed into bed and pulled up the covers, I had the strange impression that the sheets had acquired a personality. I contemplated them in astonishment. Irene, sitting naked and cross-legged beside me, an open book in her lap, reminded me with a grin that sheets always went in pairs and that they died together, like some bird species. Then her gaze wandered back to her book and she absentmindedly scratched her crotch.

Most of the discoveries we made about silence we recounted to each other in bed. In most cases they were fleeting references we had found in books on completely different subjects. One night I told Irene how in his remarkable story *The Crack-Up*, Scott Fitzgerald described his final breakdown as a vision of himself standing alone at dusk staring at a barren landscape holding an unloaded rifle, and no target to shoot at. All he could hear amid the surrounding silence was the sound of his own breathing. Fitzgerald suffered from insomnia, and insomnia was not unlike a feeling of complete and irreversible loneliness. Perhaps it was also the symptom that this loneliness was taking hold of him and that he would never get rid of it. We could perhaps write something on insomnia in general, and in particular on Fitzgerald's infinitely desolate insomnia.

One night Irene told me that among Auden's sacred beings there were four that could only be defined through non-existence: Darkness, Death, Nothingness and Silence. That was all the information she had. Our subject always came as an occasional flash of insight, but never provided us with a field of research we could

22

really get our teeth into. We would go to bed at night, and spend hours talking about silence (sometimes with great despondency), before submerging ourselves in it, both of us clinging to the sheets for fear an imaginary monster would eat them up under cover of darkness.

Irene rallied our legion of friends around two concurrent goals: finding us a job that would save us from financial ruin, and compiling information for our book. The first was accomplished swiftly and in a surreal manner. Irene was hired to script a film advertising a big insurance company. This wasn't aimed at the public at large, but rather at the company's own agents, who needed convincing that their mission, far from being that of your everyday door-to-door salespeople, was comparable to that of a guardian angel descending from the heavens onto the families whom they had to saddle with the policy. Irene went to work on the script, but it didn't prevent her from visiting the library as usual and calling up puzzled professors to ask them about reference books that had undoubtedly never been written. Over the following days, she became galvanized in a way that seemed positively frenetic when compared with my inactivity. I had decided to search for references in the books we had at home, a hit and miss undertaking if ever there was one. Thus I discovered that the first person to *produce* silence in sixteen hundred and something was a man called Sir Robert Boyle. Much to the astonishment of his fellow members of the Royal Society, he amused himself by ringing a bell inside a container where he had created a vacuum. It made no sound. I liked to imagine that one of the members of that venerable society was stone-deaf and therefore decidedly skeptical. I also learned from one of my books that the Mabaan, a primitive tribe living on the Sudanese border with Ethiopia, who had no drums or firearms, were so accustomed to silence that they spoke in whispers. I assumed this anthropological study was quite a few years old, and that the typical Mabaan nowadays was a famished black fellow sporting a Boston Celtics cap and wielding a Kalashnikov. Everything I came across was thought provoking and even poetic (like the tribe with finely-tuned hearing that spoke in whispers), but I had no idea what to do with it. I often went out for a walk to gather my thoughts, rather than stay home and admit I had none.

One morning, I returned from my walk somewhat dispirited only to discover the first message on the answering machine from one of those experts: *Irene, I got your note* (I glanced instinctively at her empty desk). The caller, a man, had a deep voice; I had no recollection of having heard it before. *Of course, there is an age-old debate as to whether sound exists or not independently of anyone being able to hear it. As you can imagine, physicists are inclined to think it exists, while philosophers are doubtful. No one expresses an opinion about silence because silence is an absence. It is considered a rather bleak and scarcely controversial field of study. In any event, whether there is such a thing as an objective sound that couldn't give a fig if anyone hears it or not, the subjective act of receiving that sound certainly does exist. The close relationship between the sense of hearing*

24

and balance suggests hearing might have evolved from the primitive balance organ of certain species of fish. This organ is a simple sac—there was a soft click and the message was interrupted. Then a bleep, and the voice resumed. *You have an impatient answering machine, darling*—darling? *As I was saying, the balance organ is a sac filled with fluid and covered in receptor cells, these cells translate the movement of liquid into nerve impulses, and this tells the fish its position in the water. Apparently these cells evolved and at some point, apart from registering the movements around them, they started detecting sound waves. What actually happened was that they became more finely attuned. Let's meet for dinner, if you like, and I'll tell you about it in more detail. Kiss, kiss.* Followed by the click.

Irene arrived home to discover that I was more intrigued by the identity of her informant than happy to know why we have an ear on each side of our head. Ultimately, realizing we had a fish to thank for our ability to hear was far less interesting than my partner's private life, to me at least. But Irene seemed unwilling to enlighten me about her friendly evolutionist. She simply protected her privacy with a mischievous smile I knew only too well that truly terrified me, because it was her way of saying it would take more than one biographer to write her life-story. Irene loved to think she would go to her grave leaving information about who she was scattered all over the place, and her greatest desire was to be different, unique, to all who knew her, as though her soul had decided that transmigration should happen simultaneously without following the normal path of successive reincarnations. Being Irene must be extremely draining, and the fact was she usually did feel very tired. A single one of her bouts of fatigue such as the one I had just witnessed when she arrived home and slumped into a chair would have provided me with two years' worth of exhaustion. And that made me feel slightly mean-minded, like someone who doesn't want to give up a privileged position for fear someone else might take his place.

And so I resigned myself to the idea of her mysterious informant writing a page of her biography, as long as it wasn't the last one. Irene rose with difficulty, put on a classical CD, and slumped back into her chair. Much to my dismay, we had nothing in particular to say to one another. That was enough to create one of those gulfs that suddenly appear in daily life that are so oppressive and poetic at the same time. Our toes were nearly touching, yet the gap between us widened until it became an immense tree-covered valley with a mighty river running through it and no boats or bridges to get across, and a wind that stirred the many centuries sedimented there. Suddenly everything seemed so ancient and alien, it was one of those magical, wonderful and terrible, moments, where distance takes control of everything. I could stretch out my arms and touch Irene, but I was afraid the gulf between us was so great that somewhere along the way my hands would turn into somebody else's.

"You know something?" Irene said, completely oblivious to the landscape dividing us, to gulfs and poetry, "a sardonic Englishman once wrote that music is the least unpleasant sound of all."

I closed my eyes and took a few deep breaths. When I opened them again, the rug was at last stretching across that impassable valley, but Irene was no longer there. I could hear her humming in the kitchen.

Although our project still hadn't taken off, at least it was useful for livening up our dinner parties. One evening a few friends came round who were too close to allow me my habitual aloofness. Irene had lit torch candles on the terrace and Rosario had prepared her signature dish: meat stew in chocolate sauce. Silvia was the first to arrive with a bottle of sherry that we opened immediately. Silvia and François had met in a café in Paris many years earlier. That winter they studied together, and ever since then they had done everything together, and yet they still refused to live under the same roof. If anyone reminded them how much their obduracy was costing, they responded as one that pragmatism was the beginning of the end of passion. Another of their habits (a result of the first) was never to arrive together. They preferred to bump into one another, in an eternal re-enactment of their first meeting in that bygone Paris café. Silvia was a quirk of nature, something that occurs on rare occasions when Mother Nature forgets her habitual vulgarity and creates something of astonishing elegance. When she sat down, even on a stool, she managed to make everyone else feel hers was the most comfortable seat. And if she walked down a flight of stairs she looked as if she were stepping lightly down a long, descending line of pedestals. Her movements were extraordinarily complicated (if we all moved like that the world would be beautiful) yet she was never putting on an act. François, who was fond of teasing, used to say that Silvia was a direct descendant of the sacred prostitutes of ancient Greece, and then give her a slap on the backside, which the rest of us found decidedly uncouth. Irene insisted that Silvia was destined to love François because he was the only man insensitive enough to treat her with familiarity. I suspected that his so-called insensitivity was the only way he could stop her from levitating everywhere she went.

That evening Silvia was glowing as if she had just swallowed a light bulb. Irene still wasn't ready, and so our friend put her arm through mine and led me out onto the terrace. It was a sultry summer evening, and in the flicker of the torch candles, I admired Silvia, an idiotic smile on my lips while she talked to me excitedly. Silvia would take my arm when she didn't know what else to do or if we had to walk into a crowded room together. And inevitably I would notice the blood rushing to the side of my body that touched hers. You might say that in some way I took up residence in that half of my body, leaving the other half uninhabited. Naturally, it made me extremely uncomfortable, but either Silvia didn't realize it or she considered it a normal reaction. Accordingly, she clasped me tighter while I grew rigid as a butler accused of drinking all the vintage burgundy. And so, ironically, although my head was filled with shameful desires flapping around like big ugly birds, at the same time it was me who felt violated while Silvia talked incessantly and gave an occasional laugh.

That evening Irene came to rescue me from my idiotic smile and my dazed, statue-like posture. She appeared at the terrace doorway dressed only in a

G-string to ask what Silvia thought of her lipstick. Our guest contemplated her with that extravagant admiration women keep for their best friends, and declared with great conviction and connivance (how could it be otherwise) that I didn't deserve her, and the two of them disappeared into the apartment. Just then, François arrived. He kissed both women on the lips (though dallied longer with Silvia) and followed them in to the bathroom unfazed by Irene's nudity. Actually Irene loved walking around without any clothes on. Our friends thought nothing of seeing her walk past them naked, usually looking for her cigarettes. And so François sat on the toilet lid with complete naturalness, while Irene and Silvia stood in front of the mirror. I gazed with pleasure at the curve of their backs and their hips, very close together, leaning against the washbasin. It occurred to me that women became more attractive when they tilted forward slightly, as they do when they put on make-up or lean against a railing or a windowsill, activities which all entail a certain self-absorption. I had a complicated thought (the sort that came easily to me), which François, enjoying the same view, summed up like a true Epicurean:

"All I need now to be perfectly happy is a glass of wine."

I went to the kitchen to uncork a bottle, but the bell rang and I made a detour and opened the door to Amador. When a bachelor approaches forty he can see being single in only one of two ways: as a privilege few of his friends still enjoy, or as an injustice he doesn't understand and that makes him feel deeply sorry for himself. The two stances are contradictory, yet, as the years go by, both become a kind of hallmark of the person who adopts them. And so the confirmed bachelor ends up vaunting his good fortune to the point where it is difficult to talk to him about anything else, while those who are like Amador ultimately derive a perverse pleasure from going to pieces all over the place. On this subject (and this subject alone, perhaps) Amador was a fanatic, and refused to let anyone deflect him from his obsessions. On seeing me he heaved a great sigh (as if to say *you have no idea how painful it is being all alone*) and I quickly dragged him to the kitchen to offer him some of the wine which François, shut in the bathroom with his wife and mine, was waiting for in order to attain complete happiness.

Soon afterward Irene and Silvia finished getting ready (Irene even wore a skin-tight dress, which was much admired) and at last we all went out onto the terrace where the torch candles were still burning. Only then did the last guest arrive, clutching a bottle of Moët in each hand, arms outstretched as if she wanted to gather us all in a universal embrace. It was our dear Olga. Olga had two children, a urologist husband whom she hardly ever saw, and several simultaneous lovers who were crazy about her. She inhabited her own exclusive world ruled by a mind teeming with ideas, all of them trivial, all of them extremely important. If anyone could get under Olga's skin for a moment, they would probably fall into a faint, overcome by an unbearable dizziness. When in company, Olga formed a bubble of the strictest intimacy with the person next to her, but would soon lose interest and happily burst the bubble only to form another one immediately afterward. She never spoke to more than one person at a time. She used to say that small talk drove her crazy, and she was only interested in people's secrets. Consequently, Olga's universal embrace was no more than her characteristically expansive way of announcing her arrival, and no more than that. She left the bottles on top of the TV set and began doing the rounds, one by one, of everybody there. Her twinkling eyes would single out her prey with the acuity of a lynx. Then, regardless of what they were doing she would grasp the victim's forearm, draw him or her away from the others and strike up a conversation, which was over so quickly that for those of us with slow reflexes it was practically impossible to get a word in edgeways. That evening the first person she waylaid was Irene, who was coming out of the kitchen carrying a bowl of salad. She steered her firmly into a corner, and wouldn't let her put the bowl down until Irene had assured her several times that she was quite well and not the slightest bit unhappy. Olga worried a lot about other people's state of mind. She then approached François, who side-stepped her interrogation thanks to his persistent habit of kissing women on the mouth (which left many a bit puzzled), so that with a worried look on her face, she made a beeline for me. I tried to back away, but bumped into the wall and was forced to proffer my arm meekly.

"Are you okay? Tell me the truth, are you feeling okay? You don't look so good."

Olga's greetings always made me feel as if I were recovering from a heart attack. Besides, my state of mind has never been unambiguous enough for me to try to describe it in any way, and the mere mention of it plunges me into instant despondency. And so I gazed at Olga with a hangdog expression. She looked terribly worried for a moment, then pounced on Amador.

As we sat down to eat, Olga began complaining to Silvia about all her women friends having entrusted her with the tiresome duty of perpetuating the species, something she did with scant maternal instinct and a husband she hardly ever saw. François let out a contemptuous guffaw for which he received a black but cordial look. Olga was good-natured. The only thing in the world that could make her angry (extremely angry) was if someone implied that her husband wasn't the father of her children, thus revealing a certain amount of moral rectitude on her part. Her lovers didn't mean much to her. She viewed them as the logical outcome of her insatiable curiosity about the opposite sex. It was Olga herself who brought up our pet subject.

"How is your book on silence going?" she asked, addressing only Irene. "I found what could be an interesting fact in the children's encyclopedia. Female cicadas' ears are located almost at the tips of their front legs. Strange place to have them, don't you think? So, when the male cicada lets out his mating call—because he won't deign to go to them, of course—the females do this with their legs (Olga spread her fingers on the table and moved her elbows from one side to the other) to find out where the lazy good-for-nothing is who wants some company. If it were me, I would never go looking for him, I'd stay right where I was gazing at the stars."

Irene looked at her slightly puzzled.

"That's interesting," said Silvia. "Now we know why some summer evenings it's like being in a mad house. The poor males are yelling their heads off and no one is paying them any attention."

I stood up in order to serve Rosario's stew. You couldn't hear cicadas from our terrace, but it wasn't completely quiet either. The city was a distant murmur on which we superimposed our own sounds. In a place like that, silence was barely more than a theory. Amador seemed to have been reading my mind.

"Montaigne said planets make a deafening roar as they rotate and move through space, only we don't hear it because we're used to it. When you drive for a long time you stop hearing the car engine. Maybe silence is just a noise we have become used to."

"At least then it would be something," I said unable to conceal a slight terseness in my voice. "Over and over, the moment we try to get closer to it, we end up analyzing something relating to sound. It's as if silence were hiding behind its opposite."

Olga looked at me as if she had just realized why I seemed so downhearted, but the smell of the stew distracted her. One of the torches flared suddenly, then sputtered and died. The moon shone palely through the plumes of smoke from the extinguished flame. François, who had remained thoughtful, lifted his fork to attract our attention.

"Maybe there's little to say about absolute silence, except that it's a total lack of sound. Relative silence, on the other hand, is much more interesting. I met a guy in Paris who liked to stay out late and who lived near the airport. The noise of the planes taking off was unbelievable, but he put up with it with great forbearance. In fact, it didn't prevent him from sleeping like a baby. My friend had gotten used to keeping rather odd hours. And that was the cause of his problem. Every night he went bar hopping until his legs, disobeying his orders, carried him home by force. When his hangover was particularly bad, he would blame them for not having brought him home sooner. One day, a couple of lovebirds who owned a florist's shop moved in to the apartment upstairs. They were early risers, and one of those methodical couples who screw every morning. When his neighbors started their fun and games, my friend had been asleep barely two hours, oblivious to the planes cleaving the air above his head. They could have been flying inside it for all he cared. But the creaking of the early morning lovers' bed woke him up instantly, and he couldn't fall asleep again until they had finished. My friend put up with the situation for a while because he was tolerant in matters of sex. But one night he arrived home tipsier than usual and couldn't stand the thought that they were going to keep him awake. He was overcome by an intense desire for revenge. He grabbed a broom and banged on the ceiling beneath their bed, letting out terrible howls. He must have scared them half to death. A while later, they started screwing with particular energy, angrily even. And so began a war of attrition. My friend would wake them up when he came home at night, and they would wake him up a few hours later. Sometimes, the lovers would fuck so violently he could hear the bed creaking even when the planes flew overhead. They never said hello if they met him on the stairs. With each day that passed the three of them became increasingly gaunt."

François paused to take a sip of wine. Night had closed in around his voice, as if the whole world had gone quiet in order to listen to the end of his absurd tale. The rest of us sat still, while our shadows danced on the table to the rhythm of the flickering torch candles.

"In the end, my friend left a note in their mailbox demanding they get a new bed, as there was no point in him changing his broom. They didn't reply. However, the following afternoon, when he returned from his frugal lunch at a local restaurant, he noticed a van parked outside the building. His neighbors, visibly weary, were unloading a huge wooden bed frame. In a sudden fit of modesty, he hid behind a tree. From that night onward the three of them went back to sleeping peacefully, lulled by the occasional rumble of airplanes."

François was right. The only possible way of broaching silence was through partial silences, those we find unbearable because we think they don't exist or because they are too overwhelming. Those silences we can't forgive or accept, the unforgettable ones. Silence only becomes interesting when it affects us, whether in a real or imaginary way. And ultimately, a book about silence couldn't be anything more than a jumbled account of how people experience silence. For want of a better way to put it: to be true to itself, our all-encompassing study had to embrace sound passionately and simultaneously shun it completely.

"I think your book is getting too complicated," said Olga, who was sitting beside me, clasping my arm with her small, pale hand. "You should write about something more tangible, something people have already written about at length. Besides, specialist literature is a synthesis of a lot of other books specializing in the same subject. And our greatest pleasure when reading it is knowing we don't have to read all the titles in the bibliography which the author was forced to plow through."

"Infidelity would make a good alternative subject," François said from the other end of the table. "It would sell really well. And with Olga around, you wouldn't need a bibliography."

Olga grunted indignantly. Not because of what François had said, but because he was in the habit of interrupting her when she was talking to someone else. She narrowed her eyes and stared straight at him. It was a sure sign that she was about to show her nasty side.

"People who talk about sex as much as you, usually don't get a lot of practice."

She turned to Silvia.

"My dear, you know you can count on me. There's more to life than conjugal duty. I'll give you the numbers of a couple of gorgeous guys. They will treat you like a princess and their conversation is always pleasant, though not particularly interesting. We don't give a damn if they're married because we don't know their wives. Go out with this smart aleck if it amuses you, that's fine, but you have to give your body what it needs. If not, you'll ruin your complexion."

As expected, Silvia didn't call Olga to take her up on the offer we all knew wasn't serious, but in an unfortunate moment of complete inner turmoil, Amador did. He must have thought he had as much right to enjoy life as everyone else, and that Olga was there to give him what he so desperately needed: a bit of casual sex. However, sex, like literature, is a fantasy one has to believe in. Amador was thrown by the complexity of things. It never occurred to him that although Olga might be promiscuous she did not consider herself an indiscriminate lover who got her kicks from being unselective about whom she slept with. In fact, the exact opposite was true of Olga. Her discernment, despite being anarchic, and quite possibly because of it, possessed the ruthless finality of a guillotine blade. I have never known anyone less swayed by the will of others. In spite of everything, she was nice to Amador. She accepted his invitation to dine with him at a very romantic seaside restaurant. Then, when Amador suggested going back to his place for a nightcap, she said she preferred to have one at a nearby bar. As they were leaving, Amador repeated his original suggestion, but instead Olga took him to a cozy cocktail lounge where they leaned on the bar and made small talk. Thus, each time they went out together and Amador tried to lure her to his freshly made bed (he had paid attention to every single detail but it hadn't crossed his mind he had to woo her) Olga would decide to have another drink at a different bar, and so his dates with her turned into a lengthy guided tour of Barcelona nightlife. Finally, when they were both quite tipsy, Olga allowed herself a shred of cruelty.

When Amador, mustering the remains of his already battered self-confidence, intimated they should finish the evening at his private wine cellar, she said he should have suggested it several hours earlier, but that it was too late now, the children had tonsillitis and her husband was probably calling the police by that time to ask them to bring her back home. She planted two noisy kisses on Amador's cheeks and gave a casual wave of her hand, as though hailing a cab by accident. And so that night, far from delivering them into the long embrace to which Amador felt entitled, ended with the glint of Olga's shoe and the soft click of the taxi door. Olga certainly knew how to make her presence felt, but she also knew how to make a discreet exit.

Amador turned up the next day, for us a pleasant Sunday, in the depths of despair. He was unshaven and wearing a long coat despite the heat. No doubt he had walked perfectly normally on his way over, yet when he came in, he was clutching a plastic bag and staggering slightly. He showed us the contents of the bag: a book, a frozen pizza and a bottle of wine. He had purchased the last two items at the grocery store on the corner, which opened on Sundays. The book was meant to show us how terribly lonely he was. He told us he had dropped by to say hello before going back home, where no one was waiting for him. Irene and I, who had just set up the barbecue on the terrace, exchanged agonized glances.

He stayed for lunch. Amador's pizza, despite my exasperated yet futile resistance (I hate frozen pizzas) took up residence in our freezer. Shortly afterward, a somewhat more cheerful Amador had lit an unnecessarily large fire, a small conflagration that threatened to incinerate the bamboo before burning Barcelona to the ground and finally blowing up the oil tankers, which were innocently sailing along the coast, unaware that Amador had decided to light our barbecue. I managed to douse the flames, but the next day our neighbor, who had been out at the time, had to re-wash the linen she had hung out on the line.

While we were having coffee, the phone rang. Irene went to answer it. Once he and I were alone, our guest's demeanor changed abruptly as he began to recount the previous night's misadventures. Gone was the constant, faintly servile smile of gratitude. At that moment he was a magnanimous man (wronged yet non-judgmental) capable of conducting a master class on the reasons behind women's fickle, indecisive nature. It struck me that such categorical wisdom was far too close to an alarming lack of subtlety. It also struck me that Olga was extremely considerate to men. I was sure dining with Amador was the last thing she felt like doing. Inviting her back to his house had added insult to injury. Olga (who owned a penthouse on La Diagonal, one of the most sought-after streets in Barcelona that would have enchanted Lord Byron, who, like her, enjoyed languishing amidst beautiful and somewhat risqué objects) found everything about her peculiar suitor repulsive. From the smell of his apartment, seldom aired, to the hallway with its assortment of earthenware jars, and the poster of revolutionary peasants in Bertolucci's *Novecento* (stapled to the wall more than fifteen years before). Walking into Amador's apartment was like embarking on a nostalgic journey into our common past. It was a place where time had come to a complete standstill. Perhaps that was why when we visited him we found it slightly depressing looking at ourselves in the mirrors and sitting on his wooden stools contemplating his bookshelves, where works by Mao intermingled with Bukowski novels and thick volumes on generative grammar. No doubt that depressing atmosphere had been too much for Amador's wife, Clara, who one fine day two years earlier had decided to run off to Nicaragua. A few months later she sent Amador a letter admitting she had shacked up with a six-foot six tall, black Sandinista. Half a year later she brought him to Barcelona to show everyone it was true, rather like Columbus had done five hundred years before. They stayed with us for ages, and Clara couldn't help often leaving him to his own devices. Johnny found it difficult to adapt to leading the life of a penniless tourist. His enormous height and prodigious energy weren't enough to prevent a persistent droop from appearing at the corners of his mouth. He began haunting Cuban dance clubs at night, despite arguing that the Cubans who washed up in Barcelona were the worst thing to come out of the Caribbean island. In fact, he only attended those dances because he knew the women who went there were looking for huge gigantic, black men like him. However, he wouldn't pick up just anyone. He was genuinely in love, and only slept with women who looked like Clara. Luckily for Johnny, his European girlfriend was rather chubby and very dark-skinned, both common features in this part of the world.

As a matter of fact, it was thanks to Olga that we met Johnny (and through him Clara and also Amador). She stumbled across him on the dance floor on one of her wild nights out on the town and didn't give up until she had succeeded in dragging him to La Casita Blanca, a discreet little hotel in the posh part of town that rented its baroque rooms by the hour. It was a disaster. Johnny ended up sobbing at the foot of the bed telling Olga how wonderful Clara was. Olga said it was the only time in her life she had wished she could exchange her delicate physique for that of a hot-blooded, well-padded, brunette.

It didn't take long for Clara to realize that Johnny was becoming increasingly drunk, tired and sadder. One fine day she yanked him out of the bed of one of her doppelgangers, they packed their bags and returned from whence they came. Amador, who had given Clara half his savings in return for keeping the apartment, discovered too late that he was still married to her. He wrote her a long, angry letter demanding legal separation. This was the same Amador who had just tried unsuccessfully to sleep with Olga, and was eager to explain to me why women were so unstable and equivocal. In fact, it was quite probable he had finished his explanation, because for a long time he had been talking and I hadn't been listening.

Irene finally emerged from the apartment. She flopped onto her chair and began gazing intently at her cup of coffee, which had gone cold. Then she stared at Amador as if she could see right through him. It looked as if she was actually examining the geranium behind our spurned lunch guest.

"That was Olga," she said, not bothering to look at him. "She's very worried about you."

That night I woke up yet again thinking I was in the hospital. More than two years had passed since they had removed the tumor, an episode that had been my own private clash with one of those silences you never forget. After so much time in the hospital, I had, without realizing it, gotten used to needing some background noise to fall asleep. I couldn't sleep in rooms that were too sealed off, where there were no disturbances to remind me I was still alive. Nor was I able to sleep alone. Irene, who knew this and supported me fully even when she was unconscious, rested in an increasingly dynamic way. Her breathing pattern changed constantly and she was continually moving. Whenever she turned over, I would reach out for her and she would clasp my hands tightly, gripping them between her thighs or covering them with warm moist kisses to stop me waking up. And yet, on some nights our dreams would drift too far apart, and we broke contact in bed. When that happened, I would return to the stuffy hospital room, permanently bathed in the half-light from the corridor, a place so calm it would emerge seamlessly at any moment from your dreams, with an sudden panic that made you open your eyes with a start. There in the hospital I had stored away somewhere in my memory a feeling of loneliness that would never leave me.

That night I was forced to face it once more, and I suspected that the reason why silence was so reluctant to reveal its transcendence was because it wanted to conceal the fact that it contained the essence of transcendence itself. My eyes opened, in the darkness. I woke up so abruptly that an intense feeling of confusion, like a spasm, coursed through my entire body. The echo of a moan I must have let out seconds before still rang in my ears. I lay still, wide awake but not knowing where I was, until I instinctively stretched out my arm and bumped into Irene's hip. She immediately turned over, searching for me with her feet beneath the sheets, but it was too late, I was back in the hospital bed. I had just had soup for dinner and was watching in silence as my roommate limped back and forth all the while complaining of a diffuse pain he couldn't pinpoint which seemed to be traveling around his body. A moment earlier, a doctor had snapped at him impatiently and asked him to calm down. We were alone. I was very still. I had grown used to not moving and I liked it. My roommate started weeping and sat down on his bed. His bed faced mine. I thought I wouldn't be able to put up with his whining much longer. Suddenly he stopped moaning, gasped as if something had surprised him, and arched his back so violently it threw him back onto the bed. The tendons of his neck stood out and he raised his clenched hands to the ceiling without taking his eyes off it. For a moment I still didn't move, astonished that he wasn't asking for my help. Then I pressed the emergency call button on my bedside table. I heard rapid clacking of heels in the corridor. A nurse poked her head round the door and the clacking receded. A moment later they appeared with a metal trolley. They pushed a tube down the man's throat. They administered electric shocks and pressed his chest, impatiently at first, then furiously, but I knew he didn't want to fight. He hadn't even asked me to help him. The doctor angrily grabbed a sheet and covered the man's face, exposing his feet. They went out of the room leaving me alone with those lifeless feet. They had completely forgotten me.

Then, once the noise in the corridor had died down, I realized just how deep silence could be, its terrifying ability to devour everything. I had the impression that the whole universe agreed with my roommate, and this was why his unmoving body radiated an overwhelming aura of certainty, as though his recent intolerable whining had found a place to vanish forever. I wanted to pull the sheet over my head, but I couldn't bear the idea of being like him, covered and lifeless. I became slowly aware of an irrational fear creeping over me, something amorphous and threatening that didn't really exist anywhere, but which can suddenly manifest itself in the feet of a man who has just died when you can't stop yourself looking at them. I started screaming, and I have never felt as alive and as terrified as I did then. Within seconds a more experienced nurse appeared and looked at me with alarm. She took my hands and held them, but I couldn't stop shaking and I begged her to do something. She understood what had happened. She could have easily sedated me, but perhaps she liked me or wasn't very busy just then. Or maybe, like me, she simply needed to fill that silence. She sat on the edge of my bed, and, still holding my hands, started telling me her life story. She spoke as if confessing to a priest, her tone dead-pan and devoid of emotion. She described her fears, the trips she had taken and the blunders she had committed, some of them unforgivable. Her words took me to an apartment in the old part of town where she was breastfeeding another woman's baby, and to a distant port watching the sunrise and discovering heartbreak, and to a dark room where the only sounds were panting and laughter. She talked on until her words began to fill the silence and my feeling of dread dissolved in that litany that resembled a desperate prayer. A fear shared is a fear halved. In the early morning, when the nursing assistants wheeled the dead man's body away, I was asleep, but I knew she hadn't let go of my hands. I am equally sure she hadn't stopped talking.

Some time later, when I was better, I sat down next to her on a bus. She didn't recognize me at first. She apologized with a distant smile. Perhaps rather casually I reminded her that she had told me her life story. The nurse shook her head and looked at me with timid eyes.

"I think I made it up," she confessed. "You can't fit all that into just one lifetime."

She thought for a moment before adding:

"At any rate, everything I told you had something to do with me in some way."

Suddenly she realized the bus was getting to her stop and she stood up nervously. I wanted to clasp her hand, but she just held it out it politely. Even so, I shook it firmly and tried to say something about her admirable story-telling skills. In the hurry, she didn't catch what I said.

"Don't thank me," she replied freeing her hand gently yet resolutely. "It's part of my job."

Our book was growing steadily longer, but we needed to structure it in some way. So far, besides the cruel fable of the sheet and the jellyfish, we had a pile of assorted quotations, the reasonable suspicion that human ears were invented by a fish, and the story of the lovebirds in the flower shop who made such a din when they screwed. And also, perhaps, the memoirs of a nurse with a fevered imagination. We couldn't even dream of reaching any conclusion with this kind of material, but that didn't really matter to us. Still, we had to figure out what to do next. The idea that our chosen subject might actually not exist, or that, if it did, its existence was strictly subjective, didn't help us in our attempts to structure our work. In the library Irene had found a study on the use of silence in public speaking, and had decided to use its index to create our own open-ended reference list for the data we had collected. Using as her guide the sublime maxim which maintains that the most beautiful silence is that which precludes any words that lack interesting content, she began to distinguish between silence that was pregnant and natural, juridical and aesthetic, respectful and ennobling, only to end up tearing her hair out when she discovered that most entries were classified under *Other Silences*.

I did my best to help her, but I had a new job that was taking up a great deal of my energy: trying to persuade someone to eat Amador's frozen pizza. Pride prevented me from throwing it away in a house where people were constantly eating me out of house and home, but I had no idea it would prove so difficult to find a willing taker. Furthermore, Rosario stymied all my attempts with her cooking. I offered the pizza to all comers—unsuccessfully—with a doggedness that made me feel pathetic. I was defeated every time by her garlic chicken, her veal rump roast, or her seabream in a salt crust, which didn't even have to leave the kitchen to defeat my pizza. Our guests, well versed in the culinary skills of the tireless Rosario, got used to to my occasionally asking them, with feigned nonchalance from my armchair, whether they felt like a pizza. The reply was invariably no. Finally I began asking without glancing up from my book—sometimes I even continued reading—so that the pizza eventually became part of every novel that I read at that time. Between the smoked ham in scallion sauce and the *plettenpudding*, the Buddenbrooks would dine on pizza using their splendid solid silver cutlery. And the much read Lolita, had pizza and coffee for breakfast while Humbert Humbert dreamed of flipping over her lithe body in order to lick her back and thighs.

That was the situation when the insurance salesmen descended on us. Irene had asked to meet one of them in order to get some idea of the target audience for her script, and five volunteers turned up after work. All five wore a dark suit and carried a leather briefcase in their right hand. They moved like a school of fish, triggered perhaps by the same nerve impulse. They seemed pleasant enough and did their best to appear extremely satisfied. Irene asked them to sit down in the living room. They accepted in a polite yet relaxed manner, as if they were distant cousins who had come to visit. I assumed that being distant cousins with everyone was an essential prerequisite of their job. I thought they must have been feeling uncomfortable since they had not yet introduced themselves. Soon they would stand up once more hands outstretched, and the rigmarole of introductions would begin. I wasn't going to be able to stomach all those smiles of nascent friendship. And so I welcomed them with a vague wave of my hand, and prepared to retire to the bedroom. Things got difficult. The salesmen interpreted my gesture as a call for silence, and they sat bolt upright in their chairs giving me their full attention. Even Irene looked at me with interest, awaiting my proclamation.

"Don't let me disturb you," I said with a catch in my voice.

I had meant to come across as forceful, but my words sounded like a standard opening line. They nodded as one, observing me with fresh interest. This made me feel almost as if I had to improvise a lengthy speech or perform a little dance for them. I decided to cut to the chase.

"I'll be in the bedroom."

I withdrew with the somewhat shaky dignity of an aging chairman of a board of directors. I had the absurd notion that as soon as I left the room they would all loosen their ties and put their feet up on the table. I stretched out on the bed, picked up a book and began to read. After a while I remembered that the pizza was still in the freezer. I felt as excited as a child. Ironic though it sounds, I was sure my excitement was a precursor of the senility that awaited me in future years. We sometimes lose sight of our true age. I felt like a capricious pig-headed old man but consoled myself with the thought that when I actually became one, I would probably feel at times like a fickle young man, bursting with vitality. In any event, it occurred to me that among all those insurance salesmen there surely had to be one willing to eat the pizza. I put down my book, made a brief stop in the kitchen and appeared in the living room holding the box in both hands in order to look more convincing. This was a disastrous tactical error. Even that pizza could have looked enticing had it been covered in piping hot, melted cheese but surely not encased in a frozen cardboard box. Stuttering slightly, I offered it to them. The salesmen rose in appreciation of my generosity, but gazed with horror at the proffered object. They were eating the leftovers of one of those superlative stews made by Rosario, our gastronomic terrorist. I decided it was time to throw in the towel. I looked at Irene, my tottering dignity intact, and solemnly announced that I had forgotten the spaghetti. She giggled. And our guests, believing they were confronted with an Italian food junkie, reassured me in unison that they weren't hungry any more.

The pizza ended up in the trashcan, which was its natural destination. Irene came to see me after a while, gave me a fleeting kiss and told me she was going out with the clones. She came home shortly before dawn. I was tired of waiting up for her so I could go to sleep. She fell onto the bed and gazed at me, her eyes filled with music. I could distinctly hear the sound flowing out of her head.

"It was fun," she pronounced. "They're normal, those guys."

Olga came round in the late morning with cockles in brine and olives. Irene was still in bed. I was holding a large cup of milky coffee, which I hadn't started drinking. Olga plucked it out of my hands and went into the kitchen to open a few beers. She popped her head round the bedroom door and called Irene. Then she breezed past me carrying a large tray so we could have the aperitif on the terrace.

Moments later we were staring at her through sleepy eyes in the shade of the bamboos. She seemed unusually nervous and was moving in a peculiar way. She crossed her slim graceful legs and began joggling her foot. She contemplated Irene with concern and looked at me with an air of annoyance. She drew a long cigarette holder out of her bag so she could smoke. Olga always behaved as if she was surrounded by beautiful people at a cocktail party on the French Riviera. She made me feel like a Carver character who has stumbled into one of the insomniac Fitzgerald's novels. I was afraid I might inadvertently spit on the floor, or drench my T-shirt in sweat. Olga appeared to agree with that impression, although I never spat on the floor or wore T-shirts. She contemplated me once more, this time with impatience.

"I wanted to see you two alone," she said. "We only see each other in crowded places."

She shot Irene a knowing look. Irene gave a prolonged yawn and turned to me.

"I met Olga at the discotheque last night. The insurance salesmen fell madly in love with her."

Our friend no longer looked concerned, but she pursed her lips in an expression of sophisticated and somewhat feigned disapproval.

"Did you tell him?" she pointed at me with her cigarette. "Does he know everything? It amazes me that you two, you lovers of silence, can't keep a wretched secret for five minutes. The fact is, I confess I came here hoping for some fun."

There were no flies on our dear Olga. She knew what she was talking about.

"When I climbed into bed with my husband this morning, I looked at him and thought I was really in love with him. He was sleeping like a baby. I couldn't understand how he could possibly love me if he knew absolutely nothing about me, if he never interrogated me or spied on me. It made me think that silence is a secret, something it is best to hide so as not to hurt others."

"Or which that someone prefers not to know so he or she doesn't suffer," Irene added adroitly.

It seemed like an interesting subject. Olga gave a loud guffaw and raised the cigarette holder to her lips. She looked at me inquiringly. She was wondering in an overt (and somewhat insulting) way whether I understood what they were talking about.

"Incidentally," she said, addressing Irene, "a couple of your admirers slept in my car. They were too drunk to tell me where they lived."

She had changed the subject. Olga found chewing over the same idea tiresome. I, on the other hand, was incapable of doing anything else. I became obsessed with the troubling silences concealed within a secret, with the idea that a degree of secretiveness was necessary even with those we loved the most. Perhaps more so than with anyone else. The closeness that comes with love could force us to hide our true selves, to obscure our despicable fears and dark desires, which might be incompatible with cohabitation. We would keep quiet in order to continue living in harmony. And the greater the love, the more passionate the relationship, the more necessary and overwhelming that silence became. Such extreme closeness would force us to feel guilty about keeping even our most trifling secrets, as if we were constantly unfaithful. And this might drive us to be really unfaithful, to relish concealing every single act of minor betrayal, those we had already committed and those we would never commit. Perhaps as time went by Irene and I concealed more and more things from each other, like someone casting off ballast to stay afloat. Perhaps it was impossible to stay together without this mounting secrecy. Couples who know too much about each other end up despising one another.

Olga carried on talking to Irene. I felt flustered and wanted to be on my own. I thought it was getting late and I still hadn't bought the papers. Irene caressed my arm without looking at me when I told them I was going out for a moment. She hadn't even heard me. I left them to it and walked down the stairs and into the street.

Once there I unexpectedly came across another unclassifiable entry for our book. The newsstand was located in a small square dominated by an ugly monstrosity of a church. The local church groupies would often pass through the square, and so there were always beggars sunning themselves on the benches, and arranging the trolleys where they kept their most treasured possessions. Nearly all the beggars spent the money given to them by the god-fearing spinsters on cheap wine they bought from a grocery store next to the newsstand, which charged twice the normal price. The storeowner, who was called Esperanza, was a dwarfish woman totally devoid of scruples. Not content with swindling the beggars, she would creep into the square at night by means of a door so tiny it looked as if it had been made so that only she could squeeze through it. Taking advantage of her customers' drunken stupor, her footsteps muffled by a pair of tartan slippers, she would scour the benches and bins, collecting any discarded bottles in a bag. She would also pick up those still containing part of the precious elixir, which she no doubt used to refill the bottles she then sold back to the beggars the following day. She would even steal bottles from the trolleys of those careful enough to stash theirs away. Thus she achieved a three-fold objective: to get money back on the empties, to cause a ruckus amongst the beggars every morning, as they pushed and shoved each other to get the money to buy her wine, and to hide the evidence of her despicable dealings from her neighbors. Only one of those exploited beggars managed to slip through Esperanza's fingers. In fact, I first met him at her store. She was leaning on the freezer cabinet, which once housed Amador's pizza. I was protesting that she had short-changed me by a hundred pesetas, while she eyed me with bogus mistrust, which was her way of feigning impeccable, and affronted honesty. Short-changing customers was another of Esperanza's usual sources of income. Just then a new beggar with an oddly relaxed, serene air came in. He said good morning to me. Then, without batting an eyelid, he turned to the shopkeeper and told her he had discovered her ploy the night before, that he regarded her as a despicable woman and that he would never set foot in her store again. Esperanza got very upset and threatened to call the police. But even her distress was a sham. When the beggar left, she walked calmly over to the cash register and gave me the fifty cents.

"He's nuts," she said jerking her head with disdain in the direction of the door. "I'll be glad to see the back of him. He only came in here to buy fruit and water."

He was well groomed for a man in his situation. He washed himself at the fountain slowly and with great care, and he carried his belongings around in a suitcase, like a traveler who has missed every train. He was a beggar who didn't beg with a wheedling voice. He usually strolled round the square reading old books he had found in the garbage. When he asked for money his tone was that of an aristocrat who has lost his way and is enquiring after a street name. If he received any money, he would strike up a conversation that could go on for as long as the donor wanted, but never to the point of becoming tiresome. He knew exactly when to remain silent, and in such cases would limit himself to a fin-de-siècle rather than an oriental curtsey. This was the man I discovered sitting on one of the benches in the square that morning. It was too soon for me to go home, but I no longer felt like being alone. It was an annoying contradiction. I hadn't struck up a conversation with a stranger in a long time. The beggar was slowly munching an apple and greeted me with a friendly gesture when I sat down beside him. I glanced at him without knowing what to say. As his mouth was full, he traced an arc above his head with the arm holding the apple to point out what a lovely day it was.

"Would you like a newspaper?" I said, fanning out the ones I had bought, like a magician displaying a deck of cards. "I've got loads here."

He waited until he had swallowed before replying.

"If you bought so many newspapers, it must be because you want them yourself."

"Take one," I insisted. "The fact is, I only leaf through them. Sometimes not even that."

He picked one at random and thanked me with a smile. He opened it out on his lap, but I carried on staring at him rather impolitely. He wasn't an anxious or stressed individual. He had the rest of his life to read that newspaper. It was my watchful presence, combined with his beggarly know-how, which made him close it again and offer me his services. He asked whether there was some way in which he could return the favor. I explained that my wife was at home exchanging confidences with a friend, and that I was working on a book on silence and didn't know how to proceed, in the same way that I didn't know what mysterious secrets my wife and her friend were enthusiastically swapping.

"It's as if I insisted on revealing in the book those secrets I'll never know," I concluded, with a somewhat tragic air.

55

He became pensive for a moment.

"You've reminded me of something that happened when I was a boy," he said. "I was twelve years old and the civil war had just ended. I was at a Catholic school in Burgos, near a village called Tardajos, where I was born. But that's another story. The school buildings were huge and it was always cold. During lessons, we hated having to take our hands out from between our thighs in order to write. Our fingers would go numb and we couldn't write properly. One of my classmates was a fat, pimply-faced boy called Pascual, the son of one of the leaders of the Movimiento, you know, Franco's nationalists. He used to sing their anthem *Cara al Sol* so loudly he drowned the others out, and he was so tone deaf the priests would gesture to him to lower his voice a little. The poor kid wasn't very bright. One day, when the priest stepped out of the classroom for a moment, to make us laugh and show us he had balls, Pascual climbed up onto the teacher's platform, gave us a defiant look, and wrote *Fuck God* on the blackboard. Then he calmly slipped back into his seat at the front of the class. A shiver ran down all our spines. When the priest came back, he stared at the blasphemy for a long time as if it were written in a foreign tongue and he couldn't decipher it. He wheeled round, the veins in his temples bulging, and demanded to know who the author was. No silence is heavier than that of a group of schoolboys refusing to betray one of their classmates. A few moments passed which seemed like an eternity. Finally, Pascual declared jauntily that it had doubtless been one of the boys in the back row. He looked at us scornfully, his eyes glinting.

There was quite a stir. The principal himself came along to demand the blasphemer's name. We were punished until further notice, break was suspended and we had to do two hours of extra lessons every afternoon. Until one day we were summoned separately before a makeshift tribunal of inquisitors, who scared us to death with terrible threats. The following day, the principal came to the classroom again to announce that an anonymous good Christian had denounced the foul-mouthed chalk-wielding apostate, and consequently sanctions were lifted. In the same breath he ordered a shy boy who was the butt of all our jokes to stand up and he expelled him from the school. We turned as one toward Pascual, who pretended not to notice. Nobody said a word, but after school that day, one of the back row's toughest boys threw a stone at Pascual's head and cracked it open. The injured boy's parents complained to the principal and the assailant was also expelled. We were at an age where nothing is more sacred than honor. Or more than honor, an implacable sense of order. We had lost two classmates, yet none of us was willing to point the finger at Pascual in order not to stoop to his level. So we took what we referred to as the Japanese decision, influenced by the world war that was going on at the time. Every break we drew straws. The chosen one that day approached the pimply fat idiot, demanded he tell the truth, then picked a fight with him. Pascual brought down two of our heroic kamikazes. The next two overcame him, but they caused so much havoc that they too were expelled. Pascual's father, alarmed by the strange hostility his son seemed to provoke, finally sent him to another school.

Only then did we conspirators choose to break our stubborn silence. The priests were bewildered by the truth, they even had a certain admiration for our cause. However, the presumption of infallibility that makes the religious establishment so mediocre prevented them from reinstating the expelled pupils. The most despicable form of silence is a failure to acknowledge one's mistakes."

Flocks of pigeons skittered round the square, alarmed by half a dozen scavenging gulls perched on the church roof. A group of wedding guests clutching handfuls of rice waited for the bride and groom to emerge from the church. They looked awkward in their finery. They glanced with alarm at the beggars who called out to them from the benches. I thought that in exchange for a newspaper this enlightened beggar had just told me something truly remarkable. Unfortunately, it wasn't much use to me either. But I started to think that silence can be the defining thing in a person's life, that each of us relates to our own silences in the same intimate, at times remote, always magical way that we relate to our own hands. I had the impression Irene and I had started work on something absurd yet fundamental.

Almost without me realizing it, silence became filled with hidden meaning. I had a feeling our approach was too superficial, that we were neglecting something deeper and more mysterious. Perhaps our subject deserved to be treated with far greater respect, with fear even, to the point where we end up behaving like whimpering dogs that crawl toward a capricious master never knowing how he would react. The most difficult secrets to penetrate are those that are clad in ordinariness. The silence we were searching for wasn't hidden in a galleon sunk in a stormy sea or in a fortress protected by obscure spells. Instead it was the silence inside a person who practiced meditation, whom Irene and I (thoughtless, pitiful reporters) approached noisily with the intention of interviewing.

I said as much to Irene one night as we got into bed. I was foolishly convinced that silence would get angry and end up taking revenge on us. Anyone else wouldn't have understood my concern. But Irene knew what it was to feel afraid and she also knew how to feel sorry for herself and others. She was experiencing something very similar. Her feelings were contradictory. The further she delved into silence the more her eyes opened. Yet the more her eyes opened, the less she could see, as though her heightened vision revealed the vast emptiness engulfing everything. Perhaps silence, which could be identified with nothingness, was right there, at the outskirts of the city, at the other side of the door, even glued to our skin, possibly caressing us with our own hands, those intimate strangers. So it wasn't a consequence of our absence after all (a tiny airtight refuge we could create unwittingly or on a whim), but rather what everything was wrapped in, it was the very air we breathed. Silence was what remains in the wake of our glittering, desperate passage, as if we were flies buzzing in a room so extraordinarily vast we will never see its walls, never produce an echo.

Irene had spent the past few days observing passers-by on the street in a mood of increasing anxiety. It was her way of meditating, which was radically opposed to mine. I sought refuge in solitude: she preferred to find inspiration amid crowds. The masturbator is as elusive as the libertine. Irene had begun to regard passers-by as small objects discarded on the ground, maybe a bit like our tiny quivering sheet. One day she took me along with her to Las Ramblas in order to explain what she felt. We sat for a long time on a bench, watching people go by. We began *personalizing* those strangers. There was a man waiting next to the subway entrance. He stood motionless staring at a floating speck in the air. Every now and then, as if someone had flipped a switch, he seemed to wake up with a start, looked up and down the avenue, and then gradually allowed stillness to overtake him once more. An old lady dressed in black, hands folded in front of her, eyes fixed to the ground, edged forward with bird-like steps. She seemed to have surrendered to a superior force, as if the world were turning slowly and she was simply doing her best to stay put in the same place. A woman walked by carrying two plastic bags bulging with groceries. She placed them on the ground for a moment, and closed her eyes, her expression unchanged, with a meekness that made you think she was closing them because when she wasn't walking she had no need of them. Irene couldn't understand why people weren't screaming or waving their arms about grotesquely in order to take up more space and to stop silence from springing up everywhere, like big empty bubbles swelling behind them with every step. Irene's vision of silence, as a mist that muffled everything we were capable of doing, was even more terrifying than the silence I had sensed, lying in wait next to us, plotting sinister revenge.

"Jesus Christ, we're so alone," she whispered beside me.

And she couldn't bear it any longer. She took me by the hand and dragged me to the nearest bar. She looked around as if she were searching for something very important she had left behind. I was familiar with Irene's occasional restlessness. We sat down at the bar and ordered two coffees. My heart was pounding out of my chest. Irene stared straight at me and slipped off the bar stool to go to the toilet. I placed one foot on the floor and waited for a while. The waiter had filled the sink with cups and plates. The crockery clattered between his fingers. I went after Irene. Her eye was awaiting me anxiously from behind a half closed door. She opened it to let me in and slid the latch across. She was naked. She got down on her knees and bit me playfully through my trousers, though there was no need. I clasped her under the shoulders and pulled her to her feet. She turned and placed one hand on the wall while the other clutched my penis, guiding me inside her. As she felt me between her thighs she let out a cry that sounded like a bomb going off. I thought someone would start banging on the door at any moment, but I didn't care. To hell with it, let them make noise if they wanted, let us all start making noise.

"Deeper," Irene panted. "Fill me up, and don't leave me, don't leave me."

I thrust my full weight inside her. My onslaught bucked her hips. Irene's naked body flattened against the tiles. She moaned as if I were hurting her, but started to lick my hand. I stuck my fingers in her mouth and grabbed her tongue. She parted her lips wide and pushed against me as if she were trying to swallow my arm, as if she needed my fingers to caress her insides. I had the vague, all too familiar, feeling that Irene was begging me for help. And I thought that, as always, I would fail her, for while I was simply enjoying being inside her (in that muffled explosion of sound) Irene was once more flirting with death.

Let us consider an example of silence by abstention, to which I was so prone, and at which I excelled at while ensconced in my armchair, taciturn but not always deaf. François worked as a publicist. This meant that he had to travel frequently to Madrid, where many of the companies employing him were based. Whenever he was away, Silvia (who lived alone but didn't know how to be alone) was in the habit of turning up at our place unannounced. As a safe-conduct, she would usually bring a bunch of flowers, a selection of cheeses or a large tub of ice cream, and would settle in as if she were at home, which she was. The truth is it never bothered me seeing Silvia draped over the sofa, or reading a magazine out on the terrace, and Irene, for her part, adored Silvia so much she thought of her as a sister. And Silvia, who was particularly gratified by feeling she was loved, took slight advantage of our admiration for her. Any type of privacy, even the slightest one, between the two of us became impossible when she appeared. And she was always present, chatting with Irene or hanging off my arm. If Irene and I were in different rooms, she would go back and forth with sheepdog-like determination until she managed to round us both up close to her. And, if we climbed into bed, she would instantly lie at our feet and start chatting to us, sprawled languorously under our admiring gaze. It bothered me slightly that Silvia came so close to me, and with such assurance, as if she were convinced that no matter what she did I would never make a pass at her. Even Olga, who had been our friend longer than her, treated me with an affectionate wariness, never for a moment forgetting I was a man. In any case, I have to confess that once, after a few drinks too many, I tried to form a secret bond with Olga by caressing her bottom. She looked at me and smiled sweetly as I fondled her, but then she took my hand and placed it on a nearby shelf as you would a paperweight, and gave me a friendly peck on the cheek. For Olga no one was neutral (she tolerated homosexuals, but had she met a eunuch she would have frantically tried to do something for him), and strangely, this allowed her to enjoy platonic friendships with members of the male sex without insulting our rudimentary vanity.

One afternoon the three of us were at home listening to Mozart. Silvia had read somewhere that researchers at an American university had just proved that listening to the Salzburg genius' music raised your IQ, and so she had brought round a few of his piano concertos played by Vladimir Ashkenazy. We preferred the Gould versions, which were the ones we had, but Irene hid them because Silvia got depressed when she brought people the wrong presents. And so we listened to Ashkenazy with an IQ ten points higher than usual (this was the conclusion the American researchers had reached), an entire afternoon ahead of us, and not much with which to occupy our over-excited minds. I sat in my armchair pretending to read whilst in fact giving in to a pleasant drowsiness. Perhaps it was true after all that Mozart made us smarter, because far from launching me into a frenzy of mental activity, an excess of mental alertness triggers in me an increasing indifference that gradually turns into a kind of drowsiness bordering on imbecility. Irene and Silvia, sitting on the carpet surrounded by books and scantily clad on that sweltering summer afternoon, were preparing a chapter of our dissertation in which we aimed to examine the relationship between silence and mythology. They looked things up in the books and talked all the time. Their voices, which seemed at once very close and very distant (as if they were coming from inside a box), combined with the champagne and oysters we had eaten (that day Silvia's safe-conduct had been especially generous) to ensure that my mental agility degenerated into to a shameful apathy. I was content to listen to them.

"For many religions sound was the first thing created," said Silvia, "even before light or air. Krishna created the world by playing his flute, the same as the Greek Goddesses with their lyres. That's how it all began. Silence was the first thing that had to be broken in order for something else to happen."

She had propped a huge volume up against the back of the sofa, and was holding the page open with an accusatory finger.

"Don't bother with that," Irene replied. "We're interested in Harpocrates now. Look him up in the index."

"He was the Greek god of silence. His statue stood at the entrance to every temple, and his image was on every seal on every letter. Some claim he was a philosopher who hardly ever spoke. That's nonsense! I've never met a philosopher who knew how to keep quiet."

I thought that Harpocrates must have been an interesting fellow, but I was too lazy to join in the conversation. Besides, it would have interrupted my practical experiment of silence by abstention, which was also interesting, although comparatively less so. Irene carried on sipping champagne. Silvia stretched, rather bored. As she raised her arms, her diminutive breasts all but disappeared, becoming two tiny hillocks on her ribcage, sensed through her blouse.

"You two are becoming a pain," she blurted out at last. "Silence doesn't exist to hide a conspiracy. All this talk about something that doesn't exist is crazy. You'll end up resembling a couple of philosophers."

Her gaze alighted on mine. A secret conspiracy, a group of plotting philosophers take a vow of silence. They aren't hiding anything. They simply decide to be quiet, to stop speaking. They become increasingly difficult to be with. They are feared because of what might come out of their mouths the day they do decide to speak. They pointlessly take up positions as public speakers and scholars. They simply nod off on their platforms, slumped over their lecterns. No one knows how many there are, because their admirers emulate them. New

65

adepts try not to open their mouths at meetings. Some become masters of the clever, penetrating gaze. The original philosophers reject this trend, but don't bother to say so. Their influence spreads like an oil stain. There is a renaissance of public interest in silent movies and their histrionic actors. Gestures come back into fashion. Crooks adopt sinister expressions, priests saintly ones. An essay that defines sincerity as the art of not attempting to explain oneself becomes a bestseller. Indifference to the word triumphs, and life becomes simpler. At that moment, the philosophers are accused of plotting a nihilistic, misanthropic conspiracy. They are proscribed, yet they don't bother to put up a defense. Due to a real lack of interest, they don't even identify with themselves. They consider their own cause derisory. They are ruthlessly persecuted. There are innocent victims. Silent bystanders are arrested and imprisoned. People become accustomed once more to thinking out loud. There is renewed public interest in televised talk shows. Everything is deemed worthy of comment, and silence is considered a disgraceful lack of ideas. A psychologist becomes renowned for arguing that deafness and dumbness are caused by apathy. Extremely violent gangs of loudmouths start to appear. Despite all this, no one manages to identify the plotting philosophers. They cunningly hide amid the hue and cry, they talk more than anyone and only spout gibberish. Someone says their ringleader has become a radio presenter. People who talk too much come under suspicion. Perhaps they are trying to cover up their true desire, which is to remain silent. Or something even worse. They are doing it as part of a new, sophisticated plot to discredit the word.

Irene shook my shoulders and Silvia burst out laughing. I looked at them as if I had just woken up from a long dream. I asked for champagne. Mozart's music really had worked devastating miracles on my brain.

It might never have happened, but many things happen for the same random reasons that glasses get broken. Americans, who are aware of this and who are also vapid and amoral, coined that astonishing maxim, which seem to be the sum total of what they have to say: you have to be in the right place at the right time. They say it, write it, chant it like a mantra with admirable sincerity, yet I have always thought that being in such a precise location can only give rise to dreadful tragedies, like being run over by a bus full of horror-struck passengers. Anyhow, apparently one fine day that summer, completely without realizing it, I decided to situate myself not in the right place, but in the perfect place. It so happened that a guy I didn't know came round one morning to pick up Irene. She hurriedly got ready, gave me a kiss so fleeting her lips didn't even touch mine, and told me in that patronizing tone women put on when they think you won't be able to survive without them, that she wouldn't be home for lunch. For a while I tried working, but found Rosario's presence particularly irksome. So I went to the bar in the square to have a beer and read the newspaper. I stayed longer than I had intended. By the time I got home Rosario had left, but a noise coming from the kitchen made me head in that direction. Silvia, a glass of water in one hand, was leafing idly through Rosario's recipe notebook (cooking wasn't a subject that interested her). Seeing me, she swept the hair from her face with a nonchalant gesture and gave a vague smile. She was wearing a white blouse and a pearl necklace that followed the contour of her collarbone. That same terrible, wonderful awkwardness I knew so well sent me into a spin. Motionless (the inevitable stupid grin on my lips), I thought that one day I might learn to banish my obsessions, or to make them real, or at least to conceal them from others. There can't be many people like me, whose inability to choose between those three options make it simply impossible for them to know what to do. Luckily, Silvia was more spontaneous, or maybe she didn't have obsessive ideas. She began talking as naturally as if she were turning on the tap. After bemoaning the fact that Irene wasn't there (blaming me with a roguish look for how hard she worked, because for Silvia money-making had a clearly masculine ring to it) she decided to stay for lunch and wait for her. She had made a date to go shopping with Irene that afternoon and wasn't willing to change her plans. She took over the house, as if she too considered me incapable of helping myself to the food Rosario had cooked. She even donned an apron and set about making a salad with somewhat brusque determination. Leaning against the marble counter, then the draining board, and then the fridge (Silvia always needed something that just happened to be behind where I was standing, and moved me aside with a discourteous little shove) I reflected that her elegant movements were like a filly's first timid steps. There was something about her limbs, about her hip joints, that made me fear she was constantly in danger of breaking a bone. At times I felt the urge to hold her in my arms, less to enjoy the feel of her body against mine than to save her from an imminent fracture. And yet she seemed perfectly content learning how to walk, and showed no sign of staying nice and still somewhere where she was most in the way, like I did. Except during her fits of rather childlike lethargy, Silvia required an astonishing amount of space to live in.

During those bouts of inertia the rest of us (me, at least) were able to obtain some respite from her, yet her lustful abandonment to boredom, innocent insofar as the most fervent whim can be, also made her excruciatingly sexy. Irene was successful with men because she unleashed in us an irrepressible desire to make her happy. Her orgasms possessed the slightly melancholic euphoria of tolling bells, of a sudden murmur of flapping wings in the forest. Silvia, on the other hand, made you want to cover her body with yours, without knowing whether you were trying to hide her from something or to hide something from her, as if there were some delicate, foul odor she needed to conceal, or to which she should never be exposed. That is what happened to me, although it might not have. Life truly is like a bus full of horror-struck passengers.

We had lunch together on the terrace then wandered away from each other for a while. Silvia began poking around the house. I cleared the table and made some coffee. She sat on the rug cup in hand, leaning back against the sofa the way she did with Irene, cursing her for being so late. There was a hint of the spoilt child in her ability to be comfortable everywhere, as though objects were shaped purely in order to accommodate her involuntary moments of torpor. During a trip to the beach the previous summer, I had watched her stretch out like an exhausted fakir on some jagged rocks where the rest of us found it difficult just to park our buttocks. If the world was full of jagged edges, Silvia possessed edges that were even sharper and of course more beautiful. Her upbringing had been very English, in the sense that the English never see a rock if what they want to see is a comfortable armchair.

Seated in an armchair, as per usual I watched her in the same way an old baboon contemplates the restive idleness of the younger members of the troop. Oblivious to her capricious invasion of my space, and stretching in the most impossible manner, Silvia also allowed herself the luxury of juggling her cup in one hand and fondling her pearl necklace with the other like a circus performer. She neither spoke nor looked at me. She had an art book precariously balanced on her lap (the book followed her movements as if someone had left it open on the ocean), and she leafed through it, the same expression on her face as when she had perused Rosario's recipe notebook, or when she looked at a fashion magazine, or read a novel. Her permanently arched right eyebrow and the perennial yawn etched on the corners of her mouth didn't diminish her intelligence, but placed her in a rather predictable way above anything that anybody could possibly try to explain to her.

It was then (without any intention of taking possession) I crouched down beside her in order to observe her more closely. Something had caught the old baboon's attention. Silvia looked at me out of the corner of her eye, but found it normal to see me beside her. It didn't affect in the slightest her happy surrender to indolence. I felt slightly irritated, I wasn't quite sure why. Absurd though it may sound, I am not sure either whether it was my irritation or a sudden fit of affection that made me do it. But I grabbed her by the chin (her jawbone dug into my palm) and planted a tentative kiss on her lips.

"Wow," she said, tersely, a smile of genuine bewilderment playing on her lips.

I had pulled away from Silvia slightly, but I was still so close I could feel her warm breath on my face. She looked into my eyes for a moment, but a confused thought made her glance away. The tip of her tongue emerged small and obscene at the corner of her mouth, and slid over her upper lip. My gut instinct kicked in. Our teeth collided with a thud and a cascade of pearls slid between us. We rolled around on the rug, the beads from her necklace sticking into us, both grunting as we struggled to tear off our clothes. We copulated with unconcealed rage (I was still irritated and it seemed to rub off on her), but also in that awkward, rather clumsy and violent way new lovers do before they get to know each other's preferences. Afterward, we crawled panting around the living room searching for the pearls, we frantically put on our clothes, terrified of being discovered, and sat facing one another gasping furiously as we tried to catch our breath. Infidelity loses part of its undeniable importance because it is so similar to a harmless act of mischief. Silvia and I looked at one another like a pair of trembling teenage accomplices. Occasionally we cast an eye over the scene of our crime to make sure we hadn't left any tell-tale signs. At last, she covered her eyes with her hand and giggled nervously. Neither of us was sure of having ever seriously entertained the idea of doing it, nevertheless we had done it.

Irene arrived soon afterward. Silvia didn't let her sit down. She accompanied her to the bathroom so that she could freshen up a bit. I could hear their muffled voices and I imagined them leaning toward the mirror. They came back arm in arm. They were going shopping and then to dinner at a restaurant downtown. I was obviously not welcome; this was a women-only night out. When they opened the front door, Irene discovered a pearl by the wall. My heart missed a beat, but Silvia took it out of her hand with a little cry of joy.

"It's from my necklace," she said. "That brute you are married to broke it."

They both turned toward me. I was prepared to hold the gaze of one or the other, but not both of them together. I suppose I failed to put on a convincing expression because they laughed. They left the house still arm in arm.

I collapsed on the sofa, and succumbed once more to a feeling of unbearable irritation. What irritated me most was not knowing why I was so irritated.

Something priceless hidden away somewhere, something which when discovered is hopelessly squandered, like a treasure in the hands of marauders. The information stored behind Irene's grey eyes was like a hidden treasure, making it extremely difficult to find out whether she knew anything or not, whether she had proof of something or was simply relying on her intuition. And, as with treasure, the secrecy about the true proportions of that information increased its value, to the point where I occasionally believed (with that exaggerated fear abysses instill in us) that there was nothing about me or the world that Irene didn't know, which was quite absurd. Besides, Irene wasn't one to boast about having discovered a secret, and that was most uncomfortable when your conscience was filthy like a sewer. There are times when you want to be found out at once, or never to be found out at all, but to ask this of Irene was like asking a snake to move in a straight line instead of a zigzag. Perhaps the image is misleading. I didn't think Irene moved in a zigzag. She was, quite simply, unfathomable.

That night she arrived home very late. I was waiting up for her in bed, reading. I wasn't fretting over the possibility of Silvia having had a sudden attack of candor, which was most unlikely. But I was going to find myself alone with Irene, and, like all petty criminals, I was afraid she would look into my eyes and be able to read my thoughts. Hiding your guilt makes you feel doubly wretched. I peered at her over the top of my book and was relieved to see she was drunk. She was propped against the doorframe, slightly cross-eyed and contemplating me with that mocking smile she always has when she is smashed. Although I had often seen her like that, her smile gave me the ghastly feeling that she knew something. Perhaps Silvia had confessed not out of remorse but because of the subtle conspiracy on which women's friendships are founded. It was possible Irene knew, but that Silvia had told her in her role as accomplice, and therefore in a mysterious, impenetrable way, amid tinkling laughter situated far above my pathetic resolve (using my book as cover) to conceal something which by then was simply another feature of their loyalty to one another. If that were true, Irene would simply laugh quietly at my ignorance, so that, in a marvelously perverse way, I would unknowingly step in to fill the vacant place of the one who has been betrayed.

Irene fell about as she undressed. She dived playfully beneath the bedclothes and snuggled up beside me. My attempts to look natural made me rigid as an inflatable doll. But her greedy hand and the touch of her skin produced a miracle I hadn't anticipated. Far from being obscured by the all too recent memory of Silvia's body (which I was afraid would overwhelm me) Irene came over as unusually intense, as if parts of her nature, which until then I had only suspected, were at last given free rein. I looked at her in astonishment, my desire so obvious that her eyes, bleary from drink, filled with flattered pride. After that she let me do what I wanted. I hoisted her on to all fours on the bed while she murmured sweet obscenities. I took her from behind with youthful fervor, digging my fingers in to her stomach as I gripped her haunches. The bedsprings started creaking as if we were a couple of impassioned Parisian florists. Inspired perhaps by that vague association with the city that has most cultivated the art of pleasure, I thought it wouldn't be a bad idea to invent a corset with handles in order to guide my beloved's hips to our mutual delight. I told her so. Irene let out a drunken guffaw, and, overcome by a sudden bashfulness, buried her face in the mattress to stifle a moan.

The following day a letter arrived for her. It had been written by a stuffy history teacher, in his late fifties, I assumed. Irene, slumped on the sofa, opened it and her eyes scanned the page. She was too hung over to read. In order to be a good drinker you have to take hangovers in your stride. Irene wasn't a good drinker. She handed me the letter with a disdainful gesture and asked me to read it out loud. I was confronted with the small, neat, fussy handwriting of someone who could have studied medicine and then, many years later, end up as librarian with a love of poetry. Irene was huddled up on the sofa, her head buried between her arms, as if she could hear the whistle of a grenade and was preparing for the explosion.

"My dear, ever esteemed friend," I read. "It is difficult to give you the information you've asked for about silence, because there would be no end to it. Silence has been a constant feature of eremitical, cenobitic and monastic life. Special attention is given to it in the Statutes drawn up by Saint Bruno, founder of the Carthusian Order. The figure of the Carthusian monk in perpetual silence has often been recorded in literature, and authors as diverse as Rubén Darío and García Lorca have written on the subject. But I shan't talk too much about the religious aspect of silence, because I don't wish to bore you, and I don't have enough years left in me to tackle such a huge challenge. As Lao Tse said: silence is the greatest strength. And Apollonius of Tyana, from a different perspective, reminded us to begin by learning that silence is also spoken word. That is how Plato's final *silentio conclusit* must be understood. As far as anxiety is concerned (why speak of Nietzsche or Kierkegaard) we need look no further than Hamlet's dying words: the rest is silence. I could fill several notebooks with references like these, but I don't think it would be of much help. So I shall permit myself to inflict one last quote on you, which I think you will find amusing, and to illustrate it with a Byzantine tale. The quote is from Sophocles' Ajax, and it is this: silence gives the proper grace to women. Don't be annoyed with me, because at this stage of the game I consider myself little more than an old buffoon. I am sure the little tale I am about to tell will appeal to you. It happened in the city of Constantinople at a time when the fate of the empire rested in Zoe's hands. She was a schemer, but I should explain that she was forced to live with her worst enemy: her brother-in-law, an ambitious eunuch. I should also say that there were many eunuchs in the Byzantine court, and they enjoyed enormous power. So this was the environment in which the sweet courtesan Armenia lived and plied her trade. Different races jostled for distinction in her oval face. And her body, if the admiration of her contemporaries is to be believed, exceeded in beauty that of any woman in the empire, which is the same as saying any woman before or since. She lived next to the Great Palace in a porticoed house surrounded by workshops that produced the city's celebrated silk fabrics. Together with her beauty, she had one other attribute that made her particularly beguiling: she was a deaf mute. Armenia attended all the courtly ceremonies, and was even said to be a frequent visitor to the throne room, where two mechanical lions made of gold would open their maws to let out a roar, and beat the floor with their tails. It seems Zoe appointed the court silencer as her protector (his task was to prevent people from talking in the emperor's presence), and so she turned into the emblem of his profession. Armenia became a kind of angelical non-presence in a place rife with conspiracy, a neutral terrain. She numbered among her clients local dignitaries, foreign ambassadors, princes of the royal household, and even, they say, the occasional church dignitary. All the men who lay with her were consumed with passion, enraptured by the sweet, smiling, exotic lips, from which no words issued. And all of them, exhausted from lovemaking, allowed themselves the pleasurable luxury of caressing her and telling her, with impunity, their darkest secrets. But by all accounts, unbeknownst to the eunuchs and even the emperor himself, wine and laughter flowed in Zoe's quarters until the early hours. Armenia, wrapped in a dark cloak, visited her mistress' bedchamber where every day the same bogus miracle repeated itself. The most monstrous secrets of the court poured from her sealed lips, and it is said that Zoe took as much pleasure from her spying as from her voice, for Armenia had the softest, most sensuous voice of any woman who had ever lived. Their secret would have remained hidden but for a general of noble spirit and athletic build. His name was Samuel. Weary after a long campaign, he sought refuge in Armenia's arms. How different Samuel was from the pot-bellied dignitaries and venerable ambassadors! Slowly, Armenia surrendered to the pleasures of Eros. As if that weren't enough, when, exhausted by his ardent lovemaking, she turned her back on the warrior, he, believing she was deaf, would confess the deepest secrets of his love for her, an all-consuming passion from which he could not escape. That was too much for our gentle courtesan. In a moment of weakness, whilst embracing the soldier, she began to whisper words of love and lust in his ear. From that moment on accounts differ. One has it that Samuel, out of injured pride, grabbed his sword and slit her throat on the spot. Another, less cruel, maintains that the alarmed courtiers had Armenia's vocal cords severed and shut her away in a convent. And yet a third claims that the courtesan and the soldier fled to a remote place outside of history, and that Zoe never forgave them for it."

Irene was still cradling her head in her arms, but within the darkness of her makeshift cave, a twinkling eye contemplated me in silence.

"In the unlikely event, my dear friend (I concluded), that you decide to use this story in your book, pick whichever ending you prefer. Fortunately for my beloved Armenia, no one will ever dispute it."

There is a fundamental difference between what you feel toward a partner you are two-timing and what you feel toward a friend you are deceiving with his or her partner. In the first case, the fear of discovery is unquestionably greater and the feelings of guilt deeper, but in the second case, you are plagued by a malaise I might refer to as *the Judas syndrome*. François, as if to rub salt on my syndrome, started being extremely friendly and nice to me. At that moment I would have preferred to see him in one of his most cynical, hedonistic moods; instead he had decided to turn sentimental. With extraordinary selfishness, I endured his increasing show of affection as something he was inflicting on me, taking advantage of my weakened position as a traitor. I knew for a fact that François enjoyed an enviable degree of freedom in his emotional life, and had never given much importance to casual encounters. That was the way my friend would have described what had happened between Silvia and me. And François himself had clocked up several dozen of them, because of his great penchant for pursuing intimate interactions with women. I felt even more indignant because the object of my unease was a man who had never suffered that malaise himself. Once again I was being unfair on him, because I knew that if I could help it my relationship with Silvia would be a bit more than a casual encounter. A few days later, I had called her with a confused desire for an encore. Silvia had told me in no uncertain terms to get a grip. Yet, true to her fickle nature, the following day she arranged to meet me at La Casita Blanca, where we were joined once more in a clumsy embrace haunted by the (ever present) ghost of our beloved Irene. This time it was Silvia who seemed irritable after we had finished. She jumped out of bed as if she had got an electric shock from the sheets. After walking up and down the room a few times, she decided we should leave separately. She dressed without looking at me and left me there on my own. I stayed in bed for a while, eagerly breathing in her perfume which lingered on me. While I was taking a shower (to remove the evidence) I had a slight feeling of loss. A lover's smell is something fresh and troubling, which, like all things, goes stale after a few hours. Perhaps it is because all trace of them is wiped away that clandestine lovers keep our desire most alive, or simply rekindle it sooner.

Irene and I were going through one of our calm periods, tinged as always with melancholy. I would often forget about Silvia completely. But there were times when, like a smoker who has given up cigarettes, I was overwhelmed by a burning urge to see her. Irene then bore the brunt of my bad temper. The result was a situation that sickened me so much I felt like saying to hell with it and confessing everything. With François things were different. The *Judas syndrome* gives rise to a state of mind based on an impossible justification, and that creates a certain hostility toward the person you are deceiving. When I embraced Silvia it was never to *hurt* Irene, but I confess I often did so (I am an indisputable villain) out of a vague desire for revenge against a friend who, although he was oblivious to what was going on, made me feel bad just by being there. And so, whenever this situation got the better of me, Irene once more bore the brunt of my ill temper, and she did so putting all her heart into it because she didn't know what was causing it.

One day around noon the doorbell rang (it was September and the weather was already cooler). My heart skipped a beat. Irene had gone out and wasn't coming home for lunch. Silvia knew that because the four of us had had dinner the previous night. It bothered me slightly that Silvia took advantage of her friend's absence to come here to see me, but I wasn't in a sufficiently rational state to reproach her for it. There are moments when you wish people would behave as ruthlessly as you would if you only dared, and yet curiously enough this doesn't prevent you from making value judgments. The world would be a very different place if we didn't tolerate our contradictions with such casual ease. So, I was even hypocritical enough to run to the bathroom and examine myself in the mirror before opening the front door with a furrowed brow that conveyed an air of moral disapproval.

It was François. He gave me a friendly hug (he must have felt he was embracing a marble column) and announced jovially that he had come round to invite me to a splendid place for lunch. I grudgingly accepted and followed him without trying to hide my reluctance. However, one advantage of appearing morose all the time is that when you really are no one notices. Once we were in the street, François placed an arm around my shoulders, and spoke to me as he patted my chest with his free hand. The usual scenario when we met was that both of us became more extreme: he is in his natural

jolliness and me in my equally natural inscrutability.
But that day the contrast was so alarming any observant
bystander would have thought a comedian had made
friends with a zombie. We arrived at the Plaza de
Vallvidrera, the whole of Barcelona at our feet, although
we couldn't see it from our table beneath a bamboo
canopy. Almost instantly François quit his euphoric
gesticulations.

"I'm a mess," he said, relishing a piece of the best
Jabugo ham, for he was quite incapable of ceasing to
enjoy the good things in life. "Last week I met a girl.
Twenty-three. Fifteen years younger than me."

I wore the expression of a benevolent *connoisseur*.
That is the expression we men always wear when our
friends reveal their weaknesses to us. What baffles me
is why we carry on revealing those weaknesses if we
already know what expression our confidant is going
to adopt. A cold breeze was blowing under the canopy
and François turned up the collar of his lightweight
jacket. My friend looked genuinely dejected. Seeing
him like that, I reflected that aging isn't the result of a
daily continuum. There are times when the weight of an
entire decade settles on our back.

"I'd never set eyes on her before. I asked her out
to dinner and she accepted nonchalantly, as if she had
nothing better to do. Then, with the same nonchalance,
she came back to my place and stripped off the moment
we entered the living room. She tossed her clothes
aside and started looking at the paintings. My God,
what a body! Yet she seemed completely indifferent to
everything around her. She was even calm when we

started rolling on the carpet. She was always *too* calm. You know? I found it unbearable. I stood up and she looked at me from the floor with a quizzical smile. I've never needed a woman to be crazy about me, but right then I wished she would clutch my legs and beg me to do whatever I wanted with her, to beat her if I felt like it. I wanted to see her topple from the heights of her insufferable calm."

The waiter brought us wild boar stew. François, who hadn't touched his wine, emptied his glass in one go and gave me a penetrating look. Not wishing to appear calm, I adopted a concerned expression. Otherwise, he was capable of flinging himself at me.

"And do you know what I said to her?"

I shrugged. The stew smelled delicious, but I didn't dare touch it.

"I said a woman like her deserved a trip to Italy, a dinner with white wine beneath a grapevine and a room looking out over the Tuscan hills. It was pathetic. As if that weren't enough, her face lit up. She jumped up and threw her arms around my neck. She thought it was wonderful, a brilliant idea. My God! Then I looked down at her large, firm breasts, nestling against my chest, her full lips and those calm eyes, with which she was, unknowingly, cornering me like an old dog. I swear it was the first time in my life I thought something was beyond my reach. I was on the verge of tears. Do you understand? There were things *I could no longer do.*"

"I've always had that feeling," I replied, venturing at last to stab a slice of wild boar with my fork. "I'm sure the moment I was born I knew it was something I could never do again."

The autumn chill was beginning to bite. We moved our little table out from under the shade of the canopy. And then, having settled in the sun, without stopping to ask myself why I was doing it, I became the biggest cynic in the world ever to break the silence of the universe with his shouting, blows and laughter.

"What I don't understand," I said, relishing my guilt, "is how you have the balls to do that to Silvia."

François gave a rueful grin. His reply would bowl me over.

"Silvia insists I go to Italy with the young lady in question. She doesn't like to think I'm not doing it because I'm afraid of losing her."

Around the same time, a miracle occurred. Amador organized a dinner at his place, which we agreed to attend with our usual steadfast enthusiasm. Irene bought two bottles of wine from Rioja, that place we never managed to set foot in, and soon after the appointed hour we wearily mounted the five flights of stairs leading to the apartment frozen in time. Amador welcomed us with a huge show of gratitude for having turned up. He knew his dinner parties were dreadfully tedious despite his culinary efforts, which produced quite acceptable results, and his splendid wine cellar, which he decimated with generous despair. He spoiled it all by embracing his role of host with excessive zeal. It is one thing to make sure your guests are comfortable and have enough chairs to sit on, it is quite another making them feel like the old maiden aunt at a family reunion who sends everyone into a frenzy of politeness. I was tired of explaining to Amador that a party is bound to be a success if you observe two basic rules: never try to force people to sit down (much less in a particular chair) and always allow free access to the fridge. But he was far too anxious to remember anything so simple, and always turned into a cross between an usher and an unbearably solicitous waiter.

However, that evening, he greeted us with a roguish smile, that, in another host would have made me think that porn movies were being shown in the dining room. The others had already arrived. Silvia and Olga, sprawled along a wooden bench against which they had protected themselves with tiny, crocheted cushions, appeared to be exchanging secrets. François was mixing dry martinis behind the hideous cocktail bar that was Amador's pride and joy. And, sitting bolt upright in a chair, her blank gaze searching for somewhere safe, a thin, pale woman silently endured what for her was undoubtedly a dreadful ordeal. Amador, renouncing his fondness for making all his guests sit down, made her stand up in order to introduce her to us.

"Behold, Natalia," Amador said behold, not this is, as if she had that very moment been created and was simply a name attached to an empty body.

Irene, true to her ability to empathize with everyone, kissed the stranger on both cheeks, instantly mimicking her posture of alarmed embarrassment. She even turned slightly pale in order to resemble her a bit more. I proffered her my hand and felt the grip of her icy fingers, which were surprisingly strong in a way that reminded me a bit of rigor mortis. We all set about frantically trying to think of something to say, until Olga came to the rescue. She took Natalia by the arm, and steered her toward the balcony, where she launched into a hypnotic speech while the other woman nodded with dignified reverence. I, who usually end up becoming an observer, realized I was standing alone in the middle of the living room. Amador had returned to the kitchen. Irene was leaning on the cocktail bar talking to a pensive François. And Silvia, still sprawled along the wooden bench, was giving me a penetrating and slightly hostile look. I hesitated for a moment before deciding to confront her. I sat down beside her and had the impression Silvia was sprouting bristles. Only her lips remained moist.

"Whenever I come near you, you turn into a hedgehog," I said in a whisper.

She smiled and the tip of her tongue appeared casually in the corner of her mouth. She instantly retracted it.

"There's something I don't like about you," she replied also in a whisper. "I haven't figured out what it is, but it's something that could drive me crazy. I wouldn't want to end up in a mental hospital because of you."

It occurred to me that I was becoming important to her, which took me slightly by surprise. I looked around instinctively for François, but he was absorbed in his conversation with Irene. When I glanced at Silvia again I realized she was watching me with pity. Then I experienced one of those moments of regression, so devoid of dynamism, where you feel like a child again with no idea of what you are doing in the world of grown ups. I felt completely disorientated.

Amador's dinner party was as boring as all the ones he hosted, despite the fact that our eyes were glued to the silent figure of Natalia, forced to sit at the head of the table, who seemed to trigger in all of us an infinite sense of disquiet. Olga did her best to fill the gaps in the conversation, but she needed François' help, and he was in a daze, perhaps preoccupied with thoughts of the young girl. Silvia had apparently decided to ignore him. She even chose to sit next to me and rested her cheek on my shoulder a couple of times. It was one of her characteristic gestures, yet on both occasions I felt uneasy and made some comment to François as though wanting to show him I had nothing to do with my own shoulder, which had somehow turned into a freakish appendage. I assume that on both occasions Silvia gazed at me again with pity, but I didn't want to know. On the contrary, I started making small talk with a fervor for which Olga must have felt thankful, as it allowed her some respite.

The surprise would come with dessert. In a last attempt to help his new-found girlfriend fit in, our host informed us she was a geologist and that she worked at the Museum of Mineralogy. Natalia demonstrated to us that even the purest white can turn pale. Her thin blood drained from her face and hands so swiftly I thought it must be circulating somewhere outside her body. Perhaps inside the chair on which Natalia was about to faint. And yet, her voice rang out clearly:

"Stones often talk to me."

Her words, hastily delivered perhaps because they were over-rehearsed, elicited a deathly silence. Habitual wisecrackers, not one of us could think up a rejoinder. As a result Natalia retreated into a sullen silence out of which no one was able to coax her. We tried in vain to include her in other conversations, as spontaneous as they were uninspiring. Possibly she was listening to the siren song of the floor tiles the rest of us simply walked on. As soon as she had finished her coffee, she stood up from the table. She took a deep breath before speaking. She announced that she had had a terrible day and needed to go home and sleep for a few hours. She picked up an enormous handbag, so full (of stones?) that when she hung it over her shoulder there was a sound of bones snapping back into place. She gave a faint smile before turning to leave the room. Amador, who had remained motionless, overcome by a kind of weary perplexity, gave a start as he heard the door click, and he ran out after Natalia. All of a sudden he remembered we were there and that he was our host. He turned toward us for a moment.

"She's terribly shy," he said by way of apology. "Almost pathologically so. I won't be long."

We heard the door slam once more, but it immediately opened again and Amador's head reappeared.

"Help yourselves to drinks. I'll be back in no time."

And off he went again. An hour and a half later, tired of nosing around among his possessions, drinking his whisky and putting up with his hard wooden benches (and having exhausted the nostalgic option of holding a revival with his old records) we decided Amador wasn't coming back, or if he was he wouldn't be thrilled to find us there. We gathered our things and turned off the lights. I was the last to leave, and the last to feel my way down the narrow, eternally gloomy staircase. As we felt for the grimy walls, we superimposed our fingerprints on those of all the people who walked up and down that staircase before us, many of whom would never do so again. It felt a bit like a forced descent into hell, albeit a necessary and agreeable one, because it was our passage to freedom. And yet we had never felt so overwhelmed as we did then by such a cruel absence of joy. I think we all had the feeling, absurd though it was, that someone was at risk.

Irene, never one to give up, arrived home the next day with a newspaper, which she opened on my lap. I ran my eyes over the pages she was showing me until I realized I had no idea what I was supposed to be looking at.

"I've placed an ad," she said. And she pointed with a trembling finger at some words framed in black like a death notice.

In those days I was feeling a bit indifferent about our book (the book we still hadn't started writing, which didn't even have the beginnings of an index), and it took me a while to identify the two anonymous researchers requesting information, stories or experiences relating to silence. I looked at Irene a little surprised. And then, as if the most stinging abuse had just issued from my lips, without moving from where she was (next to my chair) or even bothering to hide her face in her hands, she burst out crying. Irene was prone to feeling distraught and had learned to cover it up. But when she gave in to intense grief she did so in an almost passive way, revealing her terror like that little girl whose picture was taken as she fled crying from the US army down a bombed out road in Vietnam. That honesty in the midst of despair was reason enough to love her to distraction. I took her in my arms as if I were the one who needed a life-line, and there was some truth in that, because not being able to break down and cry the way Irene did made me feel almost totally worthless.

"We're getting nowhere," she sobbed in my ear. "We're growing further and further apart. We're not capable of doing anything together. Of having a baby, or going on a weekend trip, we can't even write a book together despite coming up with a brilliant idea. I can't help feeling that life is boring, and I can't handle it."

"Let's have a baby," I told her, without thinking, blurting out what seemed the most cathartic solution.

I was used to resorting to somewhat underhand methods in order to cure Irene's depressions: I would make brash proposals, which, fortunately, almost never came to anything. But this time, she turned away from me abruptly and started looking for her cigarettes.

"Never," she said emphatically. "I'll only get pregnant when I genuinely want a baby. I won't bring anyone in to this world simply because I'm not happy."

Moments later I could hear her whispering to Rosario in the kitchen. She had already bounced back (I was also amazed by her amazing ability to bounce back, for if I ever broke down the way she did I would need hospitalizing), and they were listening to the radio. Rosario maintained that because radio presenters were forced to talk non-stop, they ended up revealing important truths. Irene considered this an excellent application of the law of probabilities, and liked to help Rosario with her cooking while they waited to seize those rare pearls of the most fortuitous wisdom. It was a pleasant way to while away time. But there was only one problem. We seemed to have reached the point where even Rosario made Irene happier than I did.

Standing in the living room, it occurred to me that I was well placed to contribute an important piece of information to our elusive study of silence. What better example of it than my heinous, hidden lust for Silvia? Wasn't my silence, like most significant silences, the masking of my urge to be unfaithful? What silence could be more terrifying than a person's turbid privacy, the persistently obscure workings of their desires, their fear of trying to explain themselves and ending up making an involuntary confession? There are few things more despicable than trying to make others believe one is self-confident when one isn't. However, we all demand of others a permanent declaration of their convictions, thus forcing them, if not to lie, then at least to keep the most volatile of silences. And isn't that type of silence analogous, for reasons of survival perhaps, to the unconfessable nature of doubt? And wasn't that why Irene and I were growing apart, divided by a wedge of absolute, silent emptiness, by the most anxiety-provoking of walls, by the void?

I wished Irene and I could roll about on the beach, and, laughing uncontrollably, realize we had forgotten who we were.

Yet she still sought me out in bed while I was sleeping, her legs folding over mine, her hands caressing me in her dreams. We breathed the same heavy air over and over, and often woke up so tightly embraced that our chest and bellies were bathed in sweat. We regained in sleep the depth we lost during the day. During the night, we embarked unawares on those brief, limited journeys (toward each other) of which we were incapable in our waking life.

In part I blamed this on our bustling social life. I had never liked belonging to a group. All groups have a paranoid tendency of shutting out the world even as they draw in new converts, until the moment when they become airtight collectives desperately sucking others in. That was why I viewed with suspicion the possibility of belonging to anything. Irene on the other hand loved to be sucked in. That was precisely where she found her lifeline. Whereas I distanced myself from my friends out of a sort of ironclad indifference, Irene did so (far more efficiently) driven by her adventurous need for independence.

All of this is relevant because of what happened one late September morning. Without wishing to (in fact completely unintentionally, which shows how powerless we are to make life go the way we want) we had become a tiny clique addicted to our wretched secrets, our trifling betrayals and that inertia in the face of mutual boredom that makes us feel so close to others. It is easy in such a situation to share guilt collectively, and, what is worse, to use it to strengthen the bonds of that spurious clique. When the time comes, any excuse is good enough to unleash a storm. In our case, the victim was conveniently close at hand and played along willingly. No one can hold out against the others when they are clamoring for a tragedy.

One grim day Irene left the house very early. The same advertising agency that had provided us with an insight into the world of insurance salespeople, urgently needed information on importing various spices into Europe, and so Irene had decided to spend the morning in the library. Just after she had gone (I was still in my dressing gown and Rosario had just arrived) someone began frantically ringing the bell. I asked Rosario to open the door and I retreated to my bedroom. I could hear Silvia's flustered voice. She came in after me and dug her bony fingers into my forearms.

"I need to find Irene," she told me. "Something terrible has happened."

Moments later we were in the street hailing a cab. On the way, Silvia told me Olga's husband had had an accident. It was Olga's husband, poor guy, he was the victim! His car had veered off on a stretch of straight road, of all places, unfortunately where a steep slope went down to a dry riverbed. The car had landed on its roof, a total wreck. And Olga's husband (what was his name, again? Tomás!) was trapped inside. At that point, Silvia didn't know whether he was still alive.

At last we could rally to a good cause, struggle against adversity, and not simply surrender to our usual small-mindedness. We had been right to sense danger during our descent into hell from Amador's apartment.

We knew something was about to happen, and we knew it because we needed it. Silvia and I could now hold hands, horrified, and go find Irene together without feeling any anxiety about hiding something from her. At that moment we had far more pressing concerns. Such as purging our guilt. Who cared that we scarcely knew the victim! We were guilty because his tragedy allowed us to regain our dignity. And the fact is we put all our heart into doing so. Perhaps after this Irene would agree to get pregnant. Silvia waited inside the taxi. I climbed the gothic staircase in the library, I walked down the long aisle between the rows of computers searching for her and stormed into the reading room. A few pairs of eyes looked up. None of them belonging to Irene, who was sitting in a corner behind a pile of books. I went over to her and explained what had happened. The silence in there magnified each sound. A bald man raised a finger to his lips. Libraries are full of Harpocrates.

Our performance couldn't have been better had we rehearsed it. François arranged for a tow truck to retrieve the wrecked car. He even led the way to the riverbed where the accident had taken place. Amador picked up the children and took them to the museum where Natalia could look after them. And she, holding them close in her icy embrace, taught them how to listen to the veiled whispers of limestone, flint and porphyry rocks, until one of their relatives came to collect them. I was the one responsible for calling that relative, as well as Tomás' company, and for providing the necessary logistic support to Silvia and Irene, who, worried yet calm, did not leave Olga's side for a minute. And so, ironically, a few people whom the victim didn't have much time for took over every aspect of his life. Meanwhile, others he didn't know struggled for hours in the operating theatre to prevent him from dying. The victim had done what was expected of him and no more than that. The doctors were successful. But no one, whether out of selfishness or professional pride, could give him his legs back. The flesh that surrounded them had been left behind in the wreckage of the car.

As you might imagine, Irene's advertisement caused an avalanche of perfectly useless letters to fill our mailbox. The majority of them, prey to an unfortunately all too familiar misunderstanding, complained about all sorts of noises. We even received a few brochures from soundproofing companies. A pink envelope contained a photograph of a little girl staring doe-eyed into the camera, arms outstretched, holding a giant tortoise. She explained in shaky handwriting on a piece of notepaper that this was her pet tortoise and that its name was *Silence*. Irene placed the photograph on her bedside table. Another letter asked for money in exchange for crucial information. Someone showing a sense of humor, I admit, suggested we try screaming under a railway bridge à la Liza Minnelli while a train passed overhead. And a mountaineer (we imagined him as a sort of hermit on skis) told us that the most impenetrable, dense silence is found in a snowy landscape. We thought that was probably true and resolved to take a trip to the Pyrenees as soon as winter came. There was also a note in the form of an anonymous message, the individual letters cut out and glued onto the paper. Perhaps its time-consuming technique explained its brevity and clumsiness: *silence is where there's no noise.* As simple as that. Why keep dwelling on it? We pinned it to the kitchen door as a reminder for Rosario. Another smart aleck sent us a musical score for a bugle call for lights out made up of lengthy silences, together with a few lines explaining that the composer—himself—was a misunderstood genius. We also received several quotations from authors (one from Zenon, for example, suggesting we have two ears and a tongue to prove we should listen twice as much as we speak) as well as a few extremely pedantic mystical reflections. All who wrote in reply to our advertisement had something to offer, with the exception of one letter, whose author asked for our help. It was from the mother of an autistic boy.

"Well," said Irene rubbing her hands together. "I'm not in great shape, but I guess we'll have to go and see him."

I felt surprisingly happy that day. It was an autumn morning and a breeze was stirring the bamboo leaves. There was even a slight chill in the air and we had hurriedly lit a fire. We must have been the first to do so in the entire country. Sitting in front of the fireplace, surrounded by the letters spread out around us, I reminded Irene of my hero Italo Calvino's story about his visits to Borges. Every time they met Calvino simply sat down and said nothing. In the light of his continued silence and because his mentor was by then completely blind, someone rebuked Calvino, insisting that if this went on Borges would be unable to tell whether his friend was still there or had left. Borges leapt to Calvino's defense with his characteristic gift for retort: *Don't worry,* he replied. *I recognize him by his silence.*

We had nothing to do. No one was coming to visit or waiting for us anywhere. Irene had gone out earlier for a few minutes to buy coffee and an enormous bunch of white roses whose perfume filled our living room, which thanks to the fire had turned into a tropical paradise. Rosario, her coat on and ready to leave, told us to hurry up and open a good bottle of wine as she had prepared a splendid *suquet de peix.*

What more could we ask for?

We could have asked for a little bit of sadness, something that would spoil everything. What the hell! When you get used to destroying things, stability becomes excessively monotonous. If you go out for a stroll you end up hurrying for no reason, if you go out to dinner with a friend you end up roaring drunk ogling some poor girl with bleary eyes, if you know someone loves you, you want them to despise you. For a horse accustomed to bolting, peace and quiet is something it never had and therefore can't regain.

That was how I felt, more and more out of control yet increasingly apathetic. And to top it all, Irene had entered a phase of exasperating passivity. She went to bed each night as if it were a renunciation. I tried to read, but she tossed and turned, filling the room with anxiety. Usually she ended up taking a Valium in order to sleep.

She also became inscrutable. She came and went at all hours without telling me where she was going or what she had been doing. I didn't ask her anything, and that was the worst thing I could have done. One afternoon I realized not only had we not spoken for hours, we hadn't even glanced at each other. Sometimes I felt like a disembodied spirit haunting the house of a self-sufficient, tormented woman. She came down with flu, and that offered a short reprieve. I would bring her food on a tray and she thanked me with a smile. But she spent the hours between meals staring at the walls. I stared at a lot of walls, too, never the same ones as Irene. If one of us had a moment of rebellion and asked the other whether something was the matter, the latter would invariably say no. And the worst thing was that it was true: nothing was wrong. There are times when we seem to be waiting for something we know will never happen.

Such was my apathy that for two weeks I hadn't called Silvia; I had scarcely thought about her. Yet there was a threat of winter in the air and had we been animals we would have stirred restlessly, flaring our nostrils to sniff at strange presences. But we weren't, and so instead we contemplated the walls and read newspapers compulsively. One afternoon, I finally sensed that everything around me was collapsing. I was alone at home and Silvia showed up. She poured herself a whisky (usually she never drank) and sat down on the sofa, holding the glass between her open legs. Without knowing why, I asked her where François was. She didn't answer. She simply looked at me with the disdain of someone unmasking a cynical phony. Yet I hadn't moved. Adopting my habitual role of old baboon, all I could do was to watch her with the fatalistic longing we feel when contemplating something no longer in our reach. Silvia had never let me take the initiative. Our clandestine relationship seemed more a shameful human frailty on her part than a result of the physical attraction I felt for her. Consequently (and if we add to this my endemic penchant for inactivity and her prickly aloofness toward me) I had concluded that for Silvia the affair was over. The truth was I didn't feel all that unhappy about it. Relationships that aren't going anywhere make me uneasy, and if I was sure of anything, it was that Silvia and I would never declare undying love for each other. It was obvious we weren't even blinded by passion. And yet, there she was before me, sullen and limp, as though unable to bear my stupidly polite grin. I am a reasonably good host, although I fall short if certain courtesies are expected of me. And on that dull autumn afternoon, the courtesies Silvia was expecting of me were frankly excessive. I have never been more oblivious to someone's intentions. She was contemplating me with a seriousness that didn't bode well. Then, she looked away with annoyance and clicked her tongue.

"I don't like myself," she said in a quavering voice. "I don't like you either."

She drained her glass and picked up her bag. But instead of walking over to the door she headed toward the bedroom. She turned around briefly before going in, to make sure I was following her with that submissiveness which was, undoubtedly, what she found least attractive about me. Women like Silvia aren't interested in men who obey too easily, especially if they do so out of laziness. My pride reawakened as I realized this. I was following her, yes, but I was preparing to play hard to get. Had she flung her arms around me I expect I would have made some facetious remark. At that moment I would have preferred us to have an argument than to pretend we were casual lovers enjoying a tryst. I had forgotten that Silvia was incapable of any pretense and that what she most liked was to feel ill at ease. No one who moved her body in such a complicated way could have a personality that remotely resembled mine.

"I need you to punish me," she said.

Her eyes were trained on me like darts. She was preparing a surprise and didn't know how to do it without seeming abrupt. So she did it in the most abrupt way she knew how. She opened her bag, removed a length of thick rope, carefully rolled up, and dropped it on the bed. Once-in-a-lifetime opportunities hardly ever occur at the ideal moment. I had always thought I would give my right arm for something similar to happen to me, but that afternoon, my soul, my lungs, even my bladder were awash with autumn, such a pity. My heart began to race. Naturally, I couldn't think of any facetious remark. I was afraid. Presents scare me. Especially if I am expected to make good use of them. Moreover, I knew this wasn't Silvia's attempt to become an imaginative lover. This wasn't a game. She was forcing me to choose between running away or rising to the occasion. I opted for a cowardly compromise. I couldn't think of any other solution.

"I'll be right back," I said, and locked myself in the bathroom.

I sat on the toilet lid, closed my eyes and waited a couple of minutes. I was hoping that, finding herself alone, Silvia would decide to leave the house. There were no sounds coming from the bedroom. I stayed there as long as I reasonably could before she began to think that shutting myself in was in fact a shameful retreat. Then I opened the door.

She had undressed. She was waiting for me sitting very demurely on the bed with her hands on her knees, staring at her feet. Her jaw was quivering slightly, even though it wasn't cold. Her small nipples were sticking out like tiny telescopes. It struck me that Silvia had no right to put me to the test like this. Once again I felt angry with her. And, woe is me, I felt the urge to punish her for it. People like me end up doing out of irritation what others would do out of a deep appreciation for perversion and art.

Silvia didn't look at me again, nor did we say another word to each other. I took her by the elbow and made her stand up. She offered no resistance. I could distinctly hear her heart pounding. I pointed to the floor at the foot of the bed. She hesitated a moment, she hadn't fully understood. Finally, she knelt down and placed her arms on top of the sheets. While I was uncoiling the rope, I nudged her inner thighs with my foot. She opened her legs, resting her cheek on the bed. At that moment I could see one side of her face. Her eye was still, expressionless. Neither of us seemed to be worried that Irene might walk in at any moment. That was also part of the punishment.

I tied her knees to the bed legs. Then I slid the rope under the mattress base and pulled it out the other end. Silvia stretched her arms out and held her wrists together. I tugged hard on the rope before binding them with the slack. I rummaged through Irene's drawers for a scarf, which I used to blindfold Silvia. Not so much to unnerve her as to prevent her from seeing me. Then, just as I had feared, I took a long look at her, not knowing what to do. I wasn't a sadist. And she wasn't my slave. Besides, that same night she would be climbing into bed with François. What the hell was she doing there, all tied up, offering herself to a guy who hadn't a clue what to do with her? But Silvia was trembling and squirming slightly. She was afraid, she trusted me. I think that was the moment when I became aware that I destroyed things by default rather than (ironical though it might sound) constructively. I felt like someone in a ship's dining room in the middle of a storm, who simply watches the things slide off his table without putting them back. This put me in a bad mood. I was caught in one of the many traps energetic people set for others in order to survive. If Irene came back I too would be forced to take a stance, I had no choice but to *do something*.

I decided to get it over with as soon as possible. I took my clothes off. Once I was naked it occurred to me I shouldn't have done it. It would have been more insulting simply to unzip my fly. There was no turning back, Irene could arrive at any moment. I kneeled on the bed beside Silvia and began feeling her up. I wanted her to feel humiliated as my hands slid over her body, like those of an executioner who takes the liberty of caressing the cheek of his next victim. For heaven's sake! Any teenager in my situation would have done the same. Why did I feel obliged to take part in a ritual that made me feel ridiculous? She had let herself be tied up so that I could do whatever I wanted with her, and I knew exactly what she wanted. I leapt off the bed, knelt behind Silvia, and began fucking her viciously, with the intention of hurting her. What an absurd fantasy! She started moaning, not from pain or pleasure but rather out of impatience. Totally indignant by then, I assumed I had failed to live up to her expectations. What the hell did she want? Punishment, real punishment? Damn her and everyone hanging round my neck! I was fed up. A blind rage made me pull out of Silvia in disgust, as though I had plunged my penis into a nest of slugs. I picked my trousers up off the floor and slipped out the belt. That was how (brutalized by my rage at not knowing what to do and yet compliant) I used her to take revenge on all those who were compelling me to give up my peaceful seclusion. I struck her once (I can still hear the crack of the belt ringing in my ears), and then I struck her again, harder. Silvia's muffled cry brought me back to reality. I dropped the belt and gazed in horror at the two bright red welts criss-crossing her buttocks. For a moment I thought my heart was going to explode inside my chest. I hurled myself at her, rubbing the marks as though trying to erase them, I covered them with the most abject kisses I have ever given in my life. And then, only then, did I mount Silvia and the two of us started howling. I think we carried on howling until

I collapsed exhausted on top of her. A terrible tightness in my chest prevented me from catching my breath, but Silvia raised her haunches furiously, forcing me to pull out. I untied her hands and sat slumped over on the edge of the bed. She untied her legs by herself. She put the rope away in her bag and hurriedly got dressed.

"I hope you haven't left any marks," she said.

There was no trace of complicity in her voice. She sounded almost professional. Whereas I, just to add the finishing touch to my ridiculous behavior, felt an incredible tenderness toward her. I stood up and made as if to embrace her, but she pushed me away with a nervous gesture. She still hadn't deigned to look at me. She disappeared down the corridor. I couldn't bear it any longer. I called out to her. She turned around for a moment, she was going to grant me just a moment.

"This can't go on," I said. "We have to tell Irene."

That was how I presented it, couched in the mediocrity of the plural pronoun. I wasn't someone dangerous who could take decisions on his own. But that didn't stop Silvia from flying off the handle at my words. She roared with rage and stamped her heel on the floor.

"She's my best friend," her gaze, usually so evasive, at that moment was piercing through me. "If you hurt her, I swear I'll kill you."

She left the house slamming the door behind her. I sat down on the bed once again. On Irene's bedside table, the little doe-eyed girl was offering me her giant tortoise, as if it were a treasure. In a wild fit of remorse, I was foolishly convinced that something terrible was going to happen to that little girl because of what I'd done.

When Irene got home I shut myself in the kitchen on the pretext of preparing something for dinner. My legs were quaking. Soon afterward, the phone rang. I could hear Irene's laughter in the living room. Then the click of her heels as she drew near. She walked past the kitchen on her way to the bathroom and told me that Silvia wanted a word with me. I made my way as best I could to the phone and picked up the receiver. I didn't speak, but Silvia must have realized from the sound of my agitated breathing that I was on the other end. Her voice was neither abrupt nor professional. It wasn't affectionate either.

"You're a fucking son of a bitch. Thank you."

Perhaps I am becoming melodramatic. With hindsight, I think those were the best of times. At least we lived them to the full. At least we had something worthwhile to destroy. One day, I filled the apartment with flowers. As a result of that small gesture, Irene and I started speaking to each other again. Occasionally, when one of us was daydreaming, we would look up and catch the other's gaze. Our inertia seemed to dissolve and we felt a renewed interest in each other. Silvia was thrilled we were getting on well. She came round often, loaded with gifts as before. She and Irene would die laughing over things only they were aware of. Silvia would even slip her arm though mine like in the old days. She would give me a peck on the cheek and tell me how happy she felt. Even I felt reasonably energetic. Irene was surprised at how talkative I was when we went out with friends. One evening, after a few too many, I gave a young language graduate (I think he wanted to become a literary agent) a two-and-a-half-hour lecture on the literary panorama of our country. I expect that was enough to put him off writers forever. We all started to take vitamins. *Pharmaton* capsules were passed around like it was the trendiest drug on the market. François declared that our desire to self-medicate was the first sign that we were emerging from our autumn doldrums. He was probably right. Incidentally, he never went to Tuscany with his young girlfriend, but they did spend a long weekend together at a hotel in Caldetas. They went for walks on the beach, got things out of their system and came back rather bored. In only three days they had exhausted whatever it was they were able to give each other. Silvia could breathe easily at last. Not for a moment had she considered leaving François because of that trifling incident. And François, as though needing to justify his escapade, raved to us about the hotel and its chubby cook, a woman called Montserrat, whose Catalan sausage with prawns was second to none. Amador called to say that Natalia had moved in with him and that she was (*we couldn't imagine to what degree*) like a kind of silent geisha, always ready to wait on him, and with a voracious sex drive. He also assured us, excitedly, that in the privacy of their home, with her hair down and without her glasses, draped in the most delicate, diaphanous veil, she became as beautiful as the most dazzling Mexican fire opal ever mined from Aztec soil.

The precision of that image made us think that Natalia had begun to exercise a significant influence over his mind. Olga was the only one who didn't seem revitalized by the imminent arrival of that ominous winter. She bought her husband an electric wheelchair and the two of them shut themselves away in their apartment on La Diagonal. She would telephone occasionally. The news wasn't good. Sometimes she told us that the children couldn't bear seeing their father without any legs, they were having nightmares. Other times, she said her husband was turning into a disabled tyrant. This wasn't the Olga we knew. Even her voice had changed. She spoke in a subdued monotone. It was unthinkable that she didn't ask how we were, that she didn't demand to know everything about everyone around her (the way she always used to). Like a war correspondent immersed in some distant, bloody conflict, she limited herself to giving us a chronicle of her gradual descent into despair.

My conversation with the young linguist may have failed to awaken in him an irrepressible urge to be my agent, but it did give me back my desire to write. Our history of silence was floating aimlessly, increasingly doomed, like an iceberg swept by currents that ended up in the warm waters of the Caribbean. Even Irene seemed to have lost all interest in the book. She was terribly busy preparing a piece on the wonders of the ancient world for a travel magazine. She decorated all our walls with copies of etchings by Fischer von Erlach, Koldewey and Tempesta, showing the Hanging Gardens of Babylon, the Lighthouse of Alexandria, the Statue of Zeus at Olympia, and other lost marvels. Anybody would have thought the magazine was bringing out a special issue for would-be travelers living in Ancient Rome before the Punic wars. In fact, the idea was to show how tourism was something intrinsic to civilized man, and the source of one of his greatest pleasures. Irene devoted all her energy to becoming a kind of archaeological tourist, which distracted her considerably from her other interests. However, there I was, still fighting for our cause. Her remark about us being doomed to fail festered like a thorn piercing my heart. But an idea had occurred to me while I listened to her ramblings on the highway in Los Monegros, where we discovered the myriad possibilities silence had to offer. I resolved to write a story about a Sicilian undertaker. I wanted to set the scene in a small village near Palermo, somewhere it would be perfectly logical to think that the mafia had permeated local society. I grabbed an atlas and began to familiarize myself with the surroundings. *Bagheria* and *Monreale* were both near Palermo, but too near and too much like seaside resorts. It had to be somewhere in the interior. *Corleone* had become too notorious. *Lercara Friddi* was a tongue twister and didn't sound Sicilian enough. But maps rarely disappoint. And there it was, slap bang in the middle of the island: *Caltanissetta*. I looked it up in the encyclopedia: *Italian city, in Sicily, overlooking the Salso valley. An important sulfur mining area. Chemical and mechanical industries. Population 59,728.* Perfect! A small city at the foot of Mount Etna, where the most polluting factories sprouted like poisonous mushrooms. Moreover its sulfur production gave it a decidedly diabolical character! I imagined sinister offices where bloody revenges were plotted. That was my way of sightseeing, what the hell! I had a cast of fifty-nine thousand seven hundred and twenty-eight extras at my disposal, plus my main character: the director of a funeral home. All that remained was for me to absorb a little of the native landscape. I opened the Guide *Flammarion*. As you would expect: vast stretches of flat countryside punctuated by an occasional olive grove. Cornfields and almond trees. Travelling is so predictable! I had all I needed. The best way to start was by setting the scene. A deserted street in the outskirts of town and a trattoria with a row of sidewalk tables beneath a luxuriant grapevine. (Clichés are a shameless literary device for creating a good atmospheric setting.) Three men are having lunch in the shade. What are they eating? Back to the guidebook: Sicilian cuisine is the custodian of traditional Byzantine, Roman and Greek gastronomy. Who would have thought it? Seafood spaghetti, pasta with eggplant, salted cod, grouper and squid, all generously seasoned with aromatic herbs. I chose *caponata*, stewed vegetables in a sweet and sour sauce. And a bottle of Corvo to wash it down. Good. The three men are eating caponata and speaking in hushed tones. Something horrible had just happened. A humble parish priest, a good and holy man who always defended the poor against the exploitation of the landowners, had been found with a bullet between his eyes. Carlo, who works in the slaughterhouse, says something like: *it's the hand of the Cosa Nostra*—or words to that effect. (I will introduce my characters by name and occupation—in the time-honored tradition of Italian social realism.) *I'm going to spend the afternoon filling the hole*, Filippo adds with a grimace of displeasure. Filippo restores old paintings and bullet-riddled corpses. His technique is the same for both: he patches up the mess and then colors it in. The third man at the table keeps silent. He is the director of the funeral parlor, of course. Here I will have to give a brief description. There is no doubt in my mind that he is painfully thin. And extremely tall. No, of course not! He has to be pint-sized, like Truman Capote. With bulging eyes and sunken cheeks. And long, bony fingers. A fragile little man, prey to frequent panic attacks. He finishes his meal without saying a word, and takes his leave on some pretext. *What's the matter with you today, Stefano!* the other two say, *did someone put sulfur in your coffee this morning?* (It occurred to me that this could be a local joke.) As our man strolls through the streets, deserted at that hour, his brow is beaded with sweat. This is not due to the heat, but to a dreadful moral dilemma. Angelo, the murdered priest, was like a brother to Stefano. Together they have paid their last respects to hundreds of parishioners. Angelo was always the first to know when someone died and he would inform Stefano. Angelo was the one who brought him his customers. And now there he was, resting on the marble slab at the back of the shop waiting for Filippo to fill the hole between his eyes. So far so good. Except that Stefano *knows* who the culprits are. Two brothers, by the name of... (let's see, where is the map, a Sicilian village: *Prizzi*, heavens! *Nicosia*, no, the name should have a sinister ring, *Caltabellotta*, too grotesque, *Grotte*, that's it!) It was the Grotte brothers. Stefano knows this, but he mustn't tell anyone.

With growing anxiety, our little man prepares the chapel of rest. Here I will add some dabs of local color: the arrival of the wreaths, the professional mourners all dressed in black, a mischievous altar boy. And a few descriptions—there won't be time later. The valley stretching all the way to Agrigento and the sea. Rust-colored smoke billowing skyward. A pungent odor emanating from the sulfur plant. Calvino's smog, which evokes political corruption and the destruction of the remnants of history dotting the landscape. With that inescapable passage out of the way, I will cut straight to the main scene. Night is falling. Angelo is ready to attend his own funeral mass. Filippo has outdone himself. The corpse even possesses the beatific look of someone clearly about to ascend to heaven. Poor Stefano stands in a corner, overcome with grief. We are in the realm of silence. The murdered priest observes the absolute silence of the dead. Save for an occasional sob or whisper, the living respect the unbroken silence of the chapel of rest. And all the people of Caltanissetta are subject to the code of silence, the *omertà*. The Grotte brothers, scot-free heads bowed, arrive to pay their last respects to Angelo. Over in his corner Stefano bites his knuckles. From that moment on, a *crescendo* toward oblivion. A dark tunnel that swallows up all secrets. The helplessness of being unable to tell the truth in a place where silence is lord and master. Dawn breaks. Alone with Angelo, Stefano prepares to close the casket. On a sudden impulse he embraces his friend's dead body. A sudden impulse makes him break his silence, even if only in secret. He takes a piece of paper. With his bony fingers he writes: *Dear*

Angelo, You were murdered on the orders of the Grotte brothers. May you rest in peace. Stefano. He slips the note into the priest's lifeless hand. Bang! The thud of the lid closing. The burial. The last of the most zealous mourners disperse. The altar boy jostles the other children. Stefano returns to his place of business, dejected. Here we fast forward to the middle of the night. Our hero wakes up drenched in sweat, he feels a cold hand over his mouth. It is Angelo! It is Angelo thanking him! He goes back to sleep and has troubled dreams. In the morning, shadows under his eyes, he heads toward the bar to have his sulfur-tainted coffee. He would never get there. Sortino, captain of the *carabinieri*, summons him to his office. There he shows Stefano a piece of paper, a note someone has left on his desk overnight. Christ almighty! Mary, Jesus and Joseph! It is the note he addressed to his friend! Stefano raises his arms to heaven. *I put the note in Angelo's coffin!*, he confesses. *It's a miracle!* (The story will be written in Spanish, of course, but the original Italian words: *É un miracolo! É un miracolo!* will echo in the reader's subconscious.) Nothing short of a miracle could have broken that profound silence. And of course the inevitable happens. That afternoon, Stefano is found dead beside the gate of the sulfur factory with thirty-seven bullet holes in his body. Filippo has to deploy all his skills. The Grotte brothers pay their last respects, heads bowed. And then the final scene. Two men are having lunch at their favorite table, under the grapevine. One of them (Carlo, the slaughterhouse worker) takes a sip of wine and gently shakes his head in resignation. *Here in Caltanissetta, only the onorata società performs miracles, either that or you pay for them with your life.* THE END. It was a good idea, a little clumsy yet full of potential, the way I like them, splendid, I set to work and wrote the story in a little over five hours. Since we never finished drafting our book about silence, I ended up sending my story to a newspaper, which published it as a pleasant summer read.

Yes, there is no doubt those were good times. I had started writing again. Irene and Silvia were beautiful (I swear) and they were within my reach. What a shame that pleasure goes hand in hand with an overwhelming desire to spoil things. Now (some time later) I find myself incapable of having fun or of agonizing over things the way I used to. I suppose that is why I no longer feel the need to bring about my own destruction. I am starting to think that was the most beautiful, the only thing I had. And I wasn't alone. Somehow, strangely, we all shared that shameful need.

The only problem was that in the end we survived, and we found ourselves resenting each other because of it. How could Olga's husband still be alive when his legs were buried in a car cemetery? What did Amador think he was doing transforming a shy, mousey geologist into a geisha? Why were Silvia and I bent on unloading our shit on each other behind Irene and François' back? How could we be so *inconsequential and yet so resilient*?

Survival is a secretive, selfish, silent pursuit. It was hard to become aware of it because we usually made so much noise, and it is even very likely that we made noise on purpose. Observing a strict silence, turning unequivocally in on ourselves simply in order to survive, would have been seen by the others as puzzlingly perverse. Thanks to my determination to resume work on our book, Irene and I had the dubious pleasure of having to face a stark question of survival. The Sicilian story had left me dissatisfied. Once again I had only dallied with our subject and now I wanted to tackle it more seriously. For want of a better idea, I searched for the letter from the woman who had asked us for help. I called her. She insisted on knowing who we were and I was forced to explain that we could do nothing for her son. But that it was essential for our book that she let us see him. Perhaps she was desperate, or simply curious, in any event she agreed for us to visit one rainy November afternoon. She lived in an old one-storey house in the Gràcia district. Irene and I, huddled under our only umbrella, smiled as warmly as we could when her puffy face appeared from behind the door. The house smelled of damp, stuffy rooms. The woman let us in, closed the door and stared at us with disconsolate eyes. Then she clasped her hands in front of her and let out a deeply mournful sigh. It occurred to me that before us stood the Grotte brothers' sister. Some women who have reached a certain age enjoy acting out emotions they have doubtlessly long since stopped feeling. This was enough to make Irene hate the woman. I was sure that at that moment she hated her with a deadly hate so I hastily introduced myself before my partner decided to storm out.

The boy was in the dining room, sitting on a chair in front of a barred window. He was watching the rain, his mouth half open. It was obvious that this expression (a kind of blank astonishment) had long since taken possession of his face. He didn't turn around when we walked in to the room. The sight of him made us uneasy. Like spying on someone who is so absorbed they don't know you are there. This has happened to all of us at one time or another.

"Two years he's been like that," the woman spoke as if the boy had left the room. "He's always been a bit strange, but now it's impossible to get a word out of him. A psychologist comes three times a week. She looks at him affectionately even though he takes no notice of her. She's not very nice to me. She makes me go into the kitchen. But, when she leaves, my son is as silent as before. To be honest, I've no idea what she does with him."

She had made us some coffee. I picked up my cup and contemplated it uneasily. Everything in that house made my skin crawl. I couldn't bear the smell of sweat that impregnated everything. Irene had clearly decided her sympathies lay with the psychologist. She refused the coffee. She shot the woman an angry look and sat down opposite the boy. He continued to gaze out of the window.

"My name's Irene," she told him. "I came here to see you, not your mother."

The boy didn't even bother to blink. The woman sniggered smugly. She seemed pleased that her son was ignoring this busybody.

"Why don't you get away from here?" Irene suggested, opening up new, dead-ends in psychiatry. "You can't breathe in this house, and the world is a big place."

The woman sidled over to me. The house's odor was concentrated in her as if she were an enormous hideous perfume bottle on legs.

"If she's your wife, you'd better watch out," she whispered in my ear. "She'll dump you for the first opportunist that comes along. I know her kind. My husband used to say the same things she does."

I wanted to look daggers at her, but my infernal politeness got in the way. I wondered why a woman like her insisted on surviving, a woman who stank and did nothing except bad mouth her fugitive husband and her son who was content to stare out of a window. It occurred to me she survived out of inertia, and a kind of innate nastiness. An overwhelming desire to annoy. Meanwhile, Irene's words as she tried one last time to break the boy's stony silence rang in my ears:

"I'll come and see you again if you like. All you have to do is nod once. Just once . . ."

When we got home, I looked up an article on schizophrenia. Irene had collapsed on the sofa and was staring up at the ceiling. I was sure she couldn't grasp why someone would go to such extremes to *absent* themselves. I was worried this might plunge her into one of her depressions, so I tried to lay the matter to rest.

"Irene, it says here that, unlike the rest of us, autistic people have decided not *to hold themselves back anymore*. They have freed themselves to the point of obliterating their relationship with the world by shutting themselves off. You won't agree, but I think it's just an exaggerated way of being normal."

To my astonishment, Irene burst out laughing. She stood up and walked over to me. She hugged me tight. She covered my face with kisses.

"Don't worry about me," she said in a mischievous voice. "If women didn't exist, you'd be autistic too."

The last relatively normal gathering of our small tribe was a kind a show of solidarity with the amputee. Increasingly depressed, Olga had asked us to convince him to get out of the house. We arranged to meet them for a pre-lunch drink in La Barceloneta one sunny Sunday. There was a walkway along the seafront where her husband could practice using his wheelchair. Irene and I were the first to arrive. Then Silvia and François. We sat in the sun reading newspapers until a honking horn drew our attention. It was them. Olga had bought a compact MPV to ferry her husband around in. She waved to us feebly with her small, pale hand. Next to her, the invalid was staring straight ahead as if none of this had anything to do with him. In contrast, as soon as they saw Irene, the children clambered out eagerly, and threw their arms around her. Irene led them off by the hand to show them the beach. The rest of us helped get the wheelchair out. Then, trying to appear natural, we lifted the man up and placed him on his contraption. He didn't thank us and, an annoyed look on his face, began fidgeting, as if we had intentionally placed him in an uncomfortable position. Silvia had led Olga away and the two of them were strolling along the sea front. François and I moved forward a few steps behind them. But the man made no attempt to switch the power on, so we walked back over to him prepared to do our best to spark up a light-hearted typically male conversation. It wasn't going to be easy. François and I both let out a Sunday sigh of contentment. We exchanged despairing smiles. The invalid, oblivious to us, was contemplating the sea as if he were watching an incredibly tedious film. Then François looked with relief over my shoulder, gave a stilted laugh and announced the arrival of Amador. I turned around with exaggerated enthusiasm, but our invalid didn't catch it. I would have adopted the same attitude if, like him, I found myself in the midst of a gathering of extremely affable idiots.

Amador arrived clutching Natalia so tightly it looked as if she was propping him up. It was his clumsy way of showing her off, because they weren't alone. His ex-wife Clara had just arrived from Nicaragua accompanied by a completely different Johnny to the one we had met the year before. He was dressed in an elegant but decidedly summery white suit, and walked as if he were about to break into a tap dance at any moment. Seeing us, he gave a loud cry of joy, raising his arms and baring his enormous palms. Clara, who had remained faithful to her long linen skirts and tie-dye blouses, was wearing only a colorful woolen shawl for warmth. She had grown rather fat. To put it unkindly, she looked like a Boston feminist who had decided to *go native*.

"They're building a new country over there," she explained after we had all greeted each other. "And Johnny has become someone."

The black man gave us a proud smile.

"He's in charge of organizing the Pacific fishing fleet. There's a businessman here willing to put up the money and some second hand boats. We'll be the king and queen of sardines."

"We certainly will," Johnny added in his cheerful baritone. "And we've got our own little brown baby now. He's this high."

He bent down and placed his hand level with his knees. Then at last the invalid's voice rang out:

"Those Sandinistas, what a bunch of bastards."

Johnny looked at him for a moment without losing his smile.

"Sure thing, man. We have to show those Yankees we can live without them."

He took two strides, placing himself behind the invalid, and began wheeling the chair toward a bar with outside tables.

"And now let's have a few beers to celebrate. Johnny's shout. And you can all come to Managua whenever you like. We have a small house with a patio full of palm trees. You, too."

Still wheeling the chair, Johnny gave the invalid a few friendly pats on the chest. The rest of us swallowed hard. Olga's husband might say something so insulting Johnny wouldn't be able to shrug it off.

"I'm in no state to go anywhere," he responded to our relief a few seconds later.

"You're kidding, buddy. To get to Nicaragua you have to fly, and that's something neither of us can do. That's why we have planes, of course."

We sat down at one of the outside tables. We all drank beer, apart from Olga who ordered a gin straight up. Clara and Johnny seemed to have understood the situation, and didn't allow the invalid's bitterness to fluster them. Holding hands throughout, they were far better at filling the silences than we were. They talked about everything that crossed their minds. The children sat on Irene's knee, staring at Johnny as if they had never seen a black person before. This final gathering might have ended pleasantly, but the invalid had an ace up his sleeve. Olga swiftly emptied her glass and raised her hand to call the waiter. She ordered another gin straight up. And, then, her husband's voice rang out so stridently it was obvious he had been waiting for that moment to launch another attack.

"She's always been a fool," he said. "And now she's a drunkard as well."

We all froze for a moment, including the waiter. Irene displayed her natural presence of mind. She snorted with rage, but rose to her feet and asked the children if they wanted some potato chips. She whisked them off to the bar. Olga buried her face in her hands.

"I can't take it anymore," she sobbed. "I can't take it anymore."

The invalid went back to his weary contemplation of the sea. The rest of us looked at each other without knowing what to say. It was Johnny who found a way to respond to the attack. He turned to the waiter, who hadn't moved an inch.

"Make that a round of gin for everyone, boss."

When the drinks arrived, he stood up and emptied his in one go. He grabbed the chair of the invalid (who didn't move a single muscle) and announced they were going for a little trip. It was almost an hour before they came back. Olga's husband had turned pale and was chewing his lip. Olga had calmed down and the boys were running around between the tables. Johnny gave us his broadest smile. He rubbed his hands, stiff from pushing the wheelchair Olga's husband had refused to operate.

"Between the two of us, we've solved all of Nicaragua's problems," he said in a cheerful voice.

But we knew that during their entire walk neither of them had uttered a word. The invalid gave a feeble laugh and looked at his wife, imploring her to take him home. Nicaragua could stay as it was, and Olga too. Since there was nothing we could do to prevent it, we ordered paella, which we devoured under the pale December sun. The conversation turned to the pros and cons of Caribbean seafood.

The businessman willing to invest in Johnny's fishing fleet turned out to be an old acquaintance of Irene's. He was a small, cheerful man who wore scruffy jeans and smoked joints continuously. We bumped in to him by chance in a café one evening after leaving the cinema: he and Johnny were embroiled in discussion about an endless list of projects, Clara was looking a little bored. Irene, of course, invited them all back to our place. We sat in front of the fireplace, drinking and talking about the sea, until the sun began to filter through our frost-covered bamboo plants. The man's name was Oscar. According to Irene he had loads of money, though he looked like he had just stepped off a *Greenpeace* inflatable dinghy. I have never met a rich man less willing to show off his purchasing power. I liked him, despite Irene's apparent ability to arouse in him a dormant fascination. When he looked at her his eyes smiled without needing any help from his mouth. The situation was awkward, but only for me. Oscar adopted an attitude common to all new acquaintances who invaded our home. He decided that Irene deserved more from life than to be shut away in a place like ours with a guy like me writing a book on silence. On silence! The entrepreneur fell about laughing. What did we city-dwellers know? Silence was the melancholy landscape of the doldrums, without a single gust of wind or any sight of land, in a cramped boat with the sole company of a man who wants to kill you. He stroked Irene's foot with his hairy hand as she stretched out, dreamily. I replied rather brusquely that anyone who had read Conrad didn't need lessons on adventurous travel by sea. However (after polishing my beloved's instep a little more), he declared himself an insufferable man of action who needed to discover things for himself. That is what he said, the weasel. Irene was swooning. No doubt the cry of cockatoos and the rumble of distant drums were echoing in her head. Africa, Istanbul, Malaysia. We had all had too much to drink. I announced, raising my voice, that there was nothing in the world you couldn't find in, say, Caltanissetta. Our guests looked puzzled, but Irene giggled and planted a knowing kiss on the part of me that was closest to her, my shoulder—aching from being in unnatural position in front of the fire. I considered our tug-of-war was over, and myself the clear winner. But Oscar had remained pensive.

"Caltanissetta. It's in Sicily, isn't it? I've been there. I went round the whole island following Durrell's footsteps in *Sicilian Carousel*. I think he had done the same with a work by Eliot. I like reading novels in the places that inspired them. I remember spending a few days at a boarding house in the center of the island. I did nothing but take long walks and read *The Leopard*."

We all looked at him in astonishment, in particular Irene. He feigned embarrassment, and, as if to excuse himself for poaching on someone else's territory, he thrust home the rapier:

"Well, he who travels has more time to read than he who writes, don't you agree? Unlike the writer, who is always absorbed, the traveler combines hours of intense adventure with many hours of leisure."

Irene and Clara agreed enthusiastically. Johnny had fallen asleep. I gave a smirk, like a goalkeeper who has let an easy ball slip by him simply because at that precise moment he couldn't help sneezing.

And so we were taken over by the Caribbean dream that would prove far more enduring than our stubborn longing—if you could call it that—for Rioja.

123

To absent oneself is a way of keeping silent. To absent oneself permanently is to seek the ultimate silence. This assertion, simple as it is, sums up what, at the end of the day, will turn out to be the worst moment of our lives. We heard nothing from Olga until a couple of weeks after our Sunday aperitif. Silvia and I had become far more restrained. Rather than being crazy about each other, I think we were just so fond of each other that we liked to embrace each other in secret. It is probably foolish of me, but being with her made me feel I was with a woman who was way out of my league. Perhaps because Silvia (elegant and sleek as a filly) fulfilled to perfection that complicated habit women have when they go to bed with their lover, of showing that they are *making a gift* of themselves. And so we continued meeting at the Casita Blanca. And in that luxurious room, always welcoming and lined with mirrors like an obscene temple, she gave herself to me, and I accepted her gift with a mystical devotion. In any case, at that time the four of us went out a lot. Mostly to the cinema and to try out new places to eat. François was a real expert at seeking out Turkish or Japanese restaurants where I could hardly eat anything on the menu. It was precisely after one of those gastronomic forays (a night of indigestible Pakistani fare) that Olga suddenly turned up and everything started to fall to pieces.

It must have been very late, that hour just before dawn when the night is at its darkest. Irene was asleep next to me, but I was wide-awake, my stomach churning. I had been trying for hours to drift off to the sound of her steady breathing, when the phone rang. I sat up with a start. Then I slipped out of bed and tiptoed over to the door. I switched on the light in the corridor. Dazzled, I hurried into the living room telling myself for the umpteenth time that I must get an extension for the bedroom. I picked up the receiver and responded in a sepulchral voice. I heard her breathing (perhaps she had a moment of doubt) before she spoke.

"It's me, Olga. Can you come over? It's urgent."

I told her I'd be there in ten minutes. It was a moonless night. I couldn't even see the muted glimmer of the bamboo leaves through the window. I dressed by the light from the passageway. Irene didn't wake up, but her leg moved across the bed in an attempt to safeguard my sleep. It was cold out. I turned up the collar of my overcoat and walked the few blocks to the corner where I would be able to hail a cab. A damp, gusty wind was blowing. It wasn't long before an empty cab appeared, but the wait seemed endless at that desolate hour. I heaved a sigh of relief as I climbed in. It was stiflingly hot inside. The driver had a half-smoked cigar in his mouth, and the stuffy air (that reeked of . . . the Caribbean?) was asphyxiating. The radio was blaring from the dashboard. However disagreeable, the cab was a tiny bubble of life on a night that was to prove ice cold.

From the pavement outside Olga's building, I looked up to see if any lights were on in the penthouse. It was too high up, one couldn't see the windows from the street. I pressed the bell on the entry phone. No one answered, but the door buzzed open. I went up in the elevator thinking I was going to walk in on an unpleasant domestic scene. Instead the door was open and the house was quiet. Slightly disconcerted, I walked in, closed the door behind me and paused to listen. All I could hear was a clock ticking in a nearby room. For a moment I thought this might be something more serious than a mere quarrel. I called out Olga's name, I walked down the hallway. The kitchen light was on. I took a quick look. The lights in the living room were on. And there, sprawled on the sofa was Olga, glass in hand, grinning at me cross-eyed, her head to one side, resting on her shoulder. Splendid even at her worst, and terribly pale, she was wearing silk underwear and had slipped a peignoir over her shoulders and arms. Her eyes were red and swollen. She must have noticed my look of alarm, because she threw her head back and let out a mocking laugh. She gave a vague wave with her free hand and as she did so spilled some of the liquid from her glass. All the preliminary theatrics showed she wasn't sure of being able to speak.

"Don't worry," she slurred. "I'm on my own. That's why I'm having a party, to celebrate."

She had managed to raise her head with difficulty. Her eyes struggled to focus on me (standing before her, I saw myself once more transformed into a ghost), but her lips were still twisted into a contemptuous melancholic smile. I sat down beside her and took her hand. She snatched it away angrily, and the back of her hand struck the wall. She turned with a look of bewilderment toward where it had made contact. After a moment of apparent reflection, she lifted a leg and let it fall across mine.

"I need a man. A whole man, I mean."

I wanted to say something, but she tried to cover my mouth. Her tiny fingers collided with my cheek. Her eyes were bloodshot.

"He's gone mad. Before, he was a nice man. He didn't give a damn what I did. Now he won't leave me alone. He accuses me of sleeping with every Tom, Dick and Harry."

She was trying hard not to cry. A thread of saliva hung from the corner of her mouth. I kept quiet. I thought it was best to let Olga blow off steam.

"He says horrible things. When I go out he starts to yell at me in front of the children, says I'm going to give some black guy a blow job. Johnny, no less. I don't know what to do with him anymore."

It occurred to me their marriage had been on the rocks for a long time. There is a lot we don't know about the people we live with, but those two had decided (no doubt long ago) to ignore each other completely. But the accident had been their doom. Shut away inside those four walls, all they could do was feed the growing hatred they felt for each other.

Olga breathed hard through her nose. She ran a finger over the puffy bags under her eyes. I thought she was finally going to start crying, but she resisted.

"Do you know what the worst thing is? I haven't slept with another man since this happened. I just can't. His five star whores won't want anything to do with him now. What do I care? I have my needs like everyone else. Why the hell should I stay stuck in the same hole with him?"

"I suppose he has to get used to his new situation," I ventured. "It can't be easy."

"Fuck him. I'm not going to become the slave of some son of a bitch who's been unlucky."

She gulped down the remainder of her drink. Some of it spilled onto her chest. She passed a shaky hand across her sternum. She gave me a disdainful look.

"Take me to bed," she ordered in a shaky but stern voice. "I need some serious fucking."

I swept her up in my arms and carried her into the bedroom. The bed was a mess. Her private party must have kicked off after hours of insomnia. I set her down gently. She had lost all sense of where she was, and she stretched out, believing perhaps she had never gotten up, that everything that night, including myself, was part of the same nightmare. I took the opportunity of silently opening the drawer in her bedside table in search of some Valium. The damn drawer was empty. With any luck, she might not need it. But Olga, lying on her side with her back to me, thrust out an arm and started feeling around for me. I took her hand and sat down beside her.

"Take off your clothes," she said drowsily. "Come on."

I started caressing her from where I was sitting. She moaned slightly. I went on gently caressing her until she began to breathe more evenly. Her hand stopped misbehaving. Finally she fell asleep, but I stayed with her for a while, afraid I might wake her. I don't know why I didn't stay there watching over her all the time she was asleep. I suppose I thought it would be better not to be there when she woke up. How could I have imagined what was going to happen then? It was almost daybreak.

I hadn't thought of leaving a note for Irene, and Olga wouldn't wake up before noon. And when she did, what would be the point of seeing me there, no longer a ghost, but the remnants of a ghost she wished had never existed? I didn't mind losing a night's sleep, but watching over other people's sleep was not my idea of a good time.

I rose very carefully. I pulled the covers over her and tiptoed out. I went into the living room to switch off the lights. It was almost dawn. The house had filled with that faint glow that makes your heart sink. I switched off the kitchen light, too. As I walked down the dim corridor I saw a light under a door. It was the children's bedroom. Why the hell am I so stupidly naive and fastidious? I opened the door and a rush of anxiety winded me. That empty apartment was in fact being squatted by its own inhabitants. They had been there all the time. The children, fully clothed, slept restlessly on their beds. And the invalid, wedged in his chair, was glaring at me convulsed with rage. His jaw was trembling so violently I could hear his teeth chattering. His whole body was shaking. His arms, anchored by claw-like fingers to his stumps, flapped like rigging in the wind. Horrified, I thought this must have been the longest night of their lives. How many horrific hours of utter despair had preceded my arrival? What had driven them to scatter like castaways without leaving the apartment? Despite everything, I still didn't grasp the seriousness of what was going on. After all, I was an outsider, and I had the strange feeling of having walked into a doomed place where there was nothing to be done. The invalid wasn't looking at me with anger because I had taken advantage of the situation (he knew perfectly well I hadn't), but because I was someone just passing through, an inconvenient, inconvenienced witness, who wouldn't hesitate to save his own skin.

"She's finally fallen asleep," I told him. "Crisis over."

His eyes still fixed on me, the invalid took a deep breath. He was trying to control his shaking.

"Tomorrow is another day," I concluded.

The typical conclusion of a slightly alarmed, callous fool, who, stumbling on the aftermath of a massacre, can't get away quickly enough. Someone had to try to find a solution. But who was going to do so, if the damage was beyond repair? If there was nothing to be done, it was best to flee before you too were infected, before your only escape route was sealed off, and you ended up trapped with them in a place where misfortune was unleashing all its curses. Fear is the basest emotion. And nothing causes fear like the threat of being infected by sorrow, the profound sorrow all of us have inside us, that rat that lives in our guts, and which we go to such lengths to appease.

"Get out," he said.

He knew it too. I wasn't going to embark on his melancholy adventure. Like hell I was! Irene might wake up and I hadn't even left her a note. To be honest, I had no idea I was going to walk in on all that. Had I known, had I come prepared . . .

"Get out," he repeated in a lower, more commanding voice.

It was freezing outside. I walked for a while until a cab drove past. The city was beginning to stir. A few people were walking very close to the walls. Early-risers sitting in their cars (engines still cold, vaporous clouds billowing from the exhausts) breathed into their hands and rubbed them together. It struck me that the way cities awoke was ruthless. They didn't know the names of their inhabitants. They only needed the survivors from the day before, those who could raise anchor and start afresh, like gigantic ships incapable of ever reaching port. But I did have somewhere to go. For Goodness sake, I had a bed, one I should have stayed in. I entered the house as if I were arriving home after a long journey. Still numb from the cold outside, I undressed and climbed into bed, the coldness clinging to my skin. Irene was still asleep. Sensing me beside her she covered me with her body. I closed my eyes. And, only then did a warm pleasurable calm begin to spread through my arms and legs. A faint shiver went up my spine. The slow release. The feeling of being alive and of sinking into a thick, warm liquid. To sink. Deeper and deeper. Irene clinging to my side, Irene like a limpet preventing the undertow from sweeping away the rock she is holding on to. And finally I am caught up in a maelstrom, twisting around the hospital beds before escaping through the window into the countryside. A cool breeze on my face. Deeper. A dazzling sun, the grass growing before my eyes. Deeper, deeper. The edge of a cliff, palpitations, a wind pushing me forward then thrusting me back, the lure of the river below. Deeper, deeper. Suddenly, my heart is in my mouth, there is only the wind and a whistling in my ears, a whistling sound that grows louder and louder canceling out the other images. The fall. Only the whistling and the wind amid a terrifying darkness. Slowly, unexpectedly, the discovery of something you have long feared, panic, you try to grab hold of something, the unbearable whistling bursts in your head like a bubble, the awakening. It's over.

I sat up in bed panting for breath. I raised a hand instinctively to my chest to calm the palpitations. The telephone rang. It was daylight outside. Irene wasn't next to me. I could hear her bare feet padding down the corridor toward the living room. Then her voice, almost a murmur. I let my head fall back onto the pillow. Irene could deal with it. My legs were aching so much I was sure they would give way if I tried to get up. For a few moments, the house was very quiet. Then, Irene's footsteps returned toward the bedroom. She came in wrapped in her bathrobe, opened the wardrobe and grabbed one of my shirts at random. She threw it on the bed. She must have thought I was still asleep because she said my name a few times before she realized I was watching her.

"Get dressed," she said. "Olga's husband has committed suicide."

Back in the street, back in a cab. The driver smelled of eau de cologne. He tried to strike up a conversation, but stopped when he realized we weren't responding. Irene, silent, played with her watchstrap. I was struggling with a feeling of guilt that was like a finger jabbing at my throat. I wanted to convince myself I was right in thinking there wasn't anything else I could have done. I hadn't come up with a good watertight argument in my defense, but I was unable to see how I could have prevented it either. That man's death was so inevitable it seemed perfectly understandable. And so the best I could hope for was that Olga didn't remember what had happened. I turned to Irene.

"I was there last night," I said.

She looked at me with a faint smile. Then went back to concentrating on her watchstrap. She hadn't heard what I said.

"Irene. Olga called last night. I went over to her house. Perhaps I could have prevented it. I don't know."

She gave me a sad look. At that moment I knew, unequivocally, that Irene would have been capable of preventing it. And I also knew she was giving me a sad look because she knew it too. You could say I lacked the sensitivity to life's dramas, which Irene had in spades. Something akin to taking responsibility for a collective looming threat, against which she was permanently on the alert, and which I was incapable of even perceiving. Describing it like that might sound absurd, but while for me friends were a pleasant nuisance, for Irene they were above all people in danger whom (in some complex way I found incomprehensible) she had to protect. It struck me that my beloved was too interventionist and not sufficiently fatalistic. I didn't want to be at odds with myself for not being consumed by guilt. Moreover I had to reserve my strength, because I was afraid that with Olga things wouldn't be quite so easy to wriggle out of. And I still hadn't exhausted all possible lines of defense.

The invalid had thrown himself from one of the windows of the penthouse, but his body was no longer there. The sidewalk was strewn with sawdust. A makeshift cordon was keeping out the neighbors who had congregated around the main door. A bad-tempered policeman contemplated the onlookers and reluctantly moved them along. He gave the impression of being an usher who is bored with his job. Irene spoke to him and they let us go up to the apartment. Once again the door was open. A plain-clothes policeman, who sat smoking in the hallway, gestured with his thumb down the corridor. I moved forward with such a strong feeling of unreality that when I walked into the living room I didn't know where I was. Olga was perched on the sofa, as if she were waiting patiently for something. Her face was so puffed up that her eyes glinted like half-buried diamonds. Seeing me she groaned. I realized from the intense look of horror in her eyes that she didn't blame me for what had happened. I was merely a witness, the main witness of her guilt. I took a step toward her, but the moment she saw Irene, she stood up and ran into her arms.

"I killed him," she said, not weeping. "I did it, Irene."

The wheelchair stood in a corner. A window was open. I assumed it was the one the suicide victim had used to leap into the void. I stuck my head out reflecting that he must have really struggled to haul himself up over the railing. The thought made my stomach turn and I swung round to face the room again. Irene and Olga were still holding each other, but had moved to the sofa. The plain-clothes policeman looked at me from the other end of the room as if I had become transparent and he was simply staring out of the window. He didn't try to hide his boredom. Everything was as it should be, all of us playing our role: I was transparent again, Irene her usual dynamic self, and Olga was holding back the tears. The policeman yawned. There was a sense of things having returned to normal. That isolation ward had at last been restored to everyday life. It was a tragic outcome yet in the end a happy one, why try to deceive ourselves. An unlucky son of a bitch had had the good sense to take his leave. His departure had dispelled much of the desperate unhappiness that had been destroying that household. And the remaining inhabitants were out of harm's way. Someone had hurriedly taken the children away, and they would soon realize that things could only get better from then on. Olga was strong. She would bounce back in no time and firmly take control. Months later, lying in my arms in bed, Irene would tell me she admired Olga for the strength with which she had overcome that dreadful tragedy. And not one of us would reach the conclusion that all that had happened was that a man (an unlucky son of a bitch) had discovered one winter's night that he had no reason to stay alive. Not for others, and even less for himself. What happened would fundamentally change the way I saw things. I still thought we were amazingly resilient in spite of our insignificance. I still believed that sometimes we survived out of inertia and sometimes out of sheer spite. And yet, it was also true that survival at any price was impossible. It could happen to any of us (anyone of our friends, Irene, even me) that the sheer tenacity keeping us alive turned to sand and slipped through our fingers. Perhaps you were right (my dear, unhappy, lucid Irene), perhaps we were all in danger.

We gave him a rather hurried burial. No one shed a single tear, though we all bowed our heads, a little like the Grotte brothers. In the cemetery an icy wind was blowing which proved very convenient when it came to parting. We left him there, in the family pantheon, tucked away forever beneath a weather-beaten cherub with outstretched arms that looked like it was begging for someone to cling to him. Never has a suicide victim been so swiftly forgotten. Olga gave us all a few half-hearted kisses and climbed into the car with her lawyer. She wanted to sort out all the paperwork as quickly as possible. As it was almost Christmas, she decided to take the children to Paris. There the boys would discover that life was just as much fun as before, and even better. Their mother turned out to be a tireless, extremely lively traveling companion. They tried champagne and went everywhere with her. One evening Olga took them to the world's oldest restaurant: Le Procope. There she taught them to appreciate the traditions of gourmet dining, and explained to them what making love was. No one could doubt Olga's skill as a teacher of the art of how to be a bon vivant. In less than a month she succeeded in turning them into a pair of little men-about-town. They had no trouble spotting a Kandinsky, they knew what *en papillotte* meant, and if they saw a florist with shadows under his eyes, they would declare, amid giggles, that he was a sex addict. They sent us a photo, their arms around a fellow with a pipe who looked very much like Sartre. He was an artist friend of

François. He had taken them to see a real mummy, and never tired of telling them how beautiful their mother was. When he went off with her he would ask their permission to kidnap her for a while. The boys nudged each other.

Irene sighed with relief as she read Olga's letter. Ensconced in my armchair, I enjoyed thinking that everything was too perfect.

"That night, when I went to their house," I told Irene, "I think I became an accessory to murder."

Laughing, Irene sat on my lap. She took my head in her hands and looked at me affectionately.

"You're a sonofabitch. I forbid you from being glad if I shoot myself one day."

"Sooner or later, we all wish our lovers to die."

Silvia and François went away for a short trip. Tuscany, of course. They came back soaked with rain, sweet wine and the romantic rivalries between Guelphs and Ghibellines. They must have loved each other a lot in Italy, because for days they went round holding hands and gazing dreamily at the most mundane objects. For a moment I even suspected Silvia had forgotten all about her relationship with me. But they soon settled back in to their old routine. As for Irene and me, we were the victims of what was by then a normal lack of funds. We couldn't afford to leave Barcelona. Rosario, more maternal than ever, looked after us as if we were recovering from a long illness. That was the last time we made a concerted effort to work on our book. Shut away at home for hours and hours, the fire lit and the remains of our last meal permanently on the table, we spent hours on end trying to approach our subject, each of us from a different perspective. I wanted to write an allegorical tale about Saint John of Nepomuk, the Queen of Bohemia's confessor, sentenced to death by her husband King Wenceslas IV for doggedly refusing to reveal her secrets of confession. I wanted the secret that led to his martyrdom to be something trifling, so as to render his sacrifice all the more sublime. And I used the saint's last night in the dungeon to try to recreate the melodramatic scene in the garden of Gethsemane, with the silence of God like a massive tombstone crushing his integrity. Speak to me, O Lord, no more rest, no more silence, O Lord. I began reading the Psalms with true devotion. I imagined the beautiful, magnificent scene of a man enclosed between four dank, stone walls, his eyes staring into space (like a madman whose assertions make us tremble with fear) crying out with good reason (we knew it) *why have you forsaken me?* Why have you all forsaken me and why do You continue to forsake me? Why don't you speak? Why this overwhelming silence? What have I done to deserve this dreadful fate? And the most important question of all: Am I more evil than anyone else, or am I the victim of a hideous game of chance? It alarmed me that Saint John of Nepomuk was beginning to closely resemble Olga's husband. Whenever I tried to picture his face, I kept seeing the invalid's features. Almost without me realizing (or being able help it) the saint had turned into an embittered man. He forgot about forbearance. He wondered why he had been made to suffer such torments when his only sin was that of integrity. And all because of a foolish queen's petty secret. He was even given to fits of hysterical laughter. He started to believe that some martyrdoms had been useless and gratuitous, perhaps they all had, and he lost his faith. And with that, out of revenge, I lost my faith in him. The two of us ended up sitting on the floor of his dungeon staring resentfully at the same stubbornly mute point in space that had ruined his life and my contribution to the book Irene and I had planned to write. In brief, my story ran aground because of the mysterious silence of God, which was the very theme I was trying to tackle. I found it impossible to write coherently about a belief that was so alien to me. Nor could I find any explanation for why it was precisely Olga's husband who had lost his legs. If this was a divine plan (shut up, Nepomucene, I know what I'm talking about!), it was clearly unfair, no matter who the victim was. If it was a matter of pure chance, then who was it that insisted on remaining silent? I decided there was no solution to the problem, and that the poor saint was suffering because of my neglect. And so I threw all my notes into the wastepaper basket.

Irene's way of approaching our subject was far more abstract, but she didn't have much luck either. Her idea was a good one. It had come to her when she saw a reproduction of Munch's *The Scream. Silence is an image*, she told me. And she started collecting all kinds of strident photographs and hanging them on the walls: Dizzy Gillespie's puffed-up cheeks as he blew his horn; an enormous building at the precise moment of demolition; a crowd applauding fervently; a jumbo jet taking off with a little boy in the foreground plugging his ears . . . It got to the point where she put so many of those pictures up that Rosario fell silent. She walked around the house as if she were bailing out water on a boat full of holes. She didn't even listen to the radio. Irene became concerned and asked her what the devil was wrong with her. During all the time she was with us, that was, without doubt, the only time when Rosario (Rosario of Nepomuk?) showed any sign of revolt. She wiped her hands on her apron and looked at Irene with annoyance.

"Maybe I'm too sensitive," she said, exasperated, "but this house isn't peaceful anymore. I have the impression I've gone deaf."

And she added, unequivocally:

"I can't work in these conditions."

Irene, who believed she was creating a kind of temple to silence, something resembling the calmest place in the universe, came to the conclusion that she was in fact paying an alarming tribute to din. She responded in the same way Balzac would have if his cook had died laughing while he read her one of his dramas. She stowed her abortive collection away in a file and left it on the top shelf of our bookcase to gather dust.

That was how the Christmas vacation ended: Irene and I somewhat disenchanted with the book we had spent so much time working on for nothing, and our friends fed up with sleeping in hotels and visiting monuments. Strange though it sounds, we couldn't wait for life to return to normal. Our daily routine was beckoning us with its siren song. We wanted to *pick up where we had left off.* And then disaster struck.

We missed a perfect opportunity to bury everything we were neither satisfied nor sure about in the old year, along with the memory of Olga's husband. Not that we had much choice, for there are some things you can't give up without running the risk of turning them into something important. If Silvia had told me that she wanted to end our affair, I would have accepted without a word, and even with a slight sense of relief. However, it is one thing to stoically accept an inevitable loss, and quite another to give up something simply because of the intrusion of a moral argument one isn't entirely convinced of. I imagine Silvia felt the same way, which made it almost impossible for us not to continue being lovers. How many couples stay together despite sharing a secret desire to be abandoned! And so I was practically compelled, one night all four of us went out to dinner (at a dreadful Mexican restaurant with photographs of Pancho Villa and greasy guitars hanging on the walls), to find a quiet moment to tell Silvia I had to see her. She looked straight at me for a few seconds. Her restless fingers flicked the ash from her cigarette. She must have been silently cursing herself for being so attractive to me, but she wasn't about to take the first step that would place upon her shoulders the onus to end things.

"Me too," she said rather sharply.

A favorable situation came up almost immediately, and it would have been almost churlish not to take advantage of it. François announced he was going to Madrid for a few days. Silvia made a face, and, despite our presence, asked him point blank if he was taking some young girl with him. Irene and I developed a sudden interest in the food on our plates. She was being unfair. François had never hidden anything from her, and it was preposterous to imagine he would choose that precise evening to start doing so. I had always thought that (unlike Olga and her late husband) Silvia and François stayed together *in spite of* his occasional brutal frankness. Silvia was unfazed by François' boorish behavior. Her indifference to his frequent infidelities seemed to come from a kind of fatalistic masochism (more of a female thing, incidentally) rather than from a pact of non-aggression between two radical free spirits. Silvia was very different from her partner. Notwithstanding our affair, no one was aware of her having had even the briefest of dalliances. And it was obvious she kept our relationship a secret as if (rather than a betrayal) it were a threat to the natural order of things. That evening, François laughed loudly and told her she had decided to turn jealous on him just when he was beginning to behave himself. Silvia swore at him with obvious tenderness, and Irene and I were finally able to look up from our plates. In my case, this was a true liberation, as they had served me a plate of Mexican meat and onions that seemed to have been scraped off the floor of a pigsty.

That night, lying in bed, Irene was reading the newspaper while I skimmed through a novel that hadn't managed to hold my interest. I let it fall on my lap and lay gazing at the ceiling. Then I realized Irene had been doing the same thing for a while.

"I'm going to ask François to give me a lift to Madrid," she said. "He's going by car so it won't cost me anything. I'll visit a few publishers and take the opportunity to clear my head a bit."

We carried on staring at the ceiling. Neither of us had turned toward the other. We were like one of those married couples who describe their day to each other eyes glued to the television. It didn't surprise me that Irene hadn't invited me on her little getaway. It was very much in character, and understandable after spending the entire vacation stuck in the apartment without seeing anyone except Rosario. All I could think of was that, for the first time since we became lovers, Silvia and I were going to be alone in Barcelona. The thought made me feel slightly dizzy. This was no longer about meeting up for a few hours to make love and then rushing off. We would have time to enjoy *being a couple for a while*. Entire nights. And breakfast, that dangerous moment when lovers find out how much in love they really are. It was going to be something of a trial, but one that was perhaps necessary for us to find out whether we wanted to go on seeing each other in secret. As François knew from experience, a couple of days living together were enough to stifle a passionate love that had initially seemed eternal.

And yet, I couldn't deny that this impeccable rationalization was no more than an excuse. And I needed it in order to convince myself that by spending a few days measuring the extent of our mutual dependence, Silvia and I were not simply committing one more crime of lèse-amity, but were instead doing our respective partners a tremendous favor. What more could we do for them than risk getting fed up with each other? Lying in bed beside Irene, without taking my eyes off the ceiling, I felt almost *forced* to jeopardize my relationship with Silvia. Even a dozy brain like mine is sometimes capable of an immeasurably good deed.

The day came for them to leave. François arrived very early to pick up Irene. I was still in bed, but I put on my bathrobe and went to say goodbye to them. Irene looked happy. She was wearing perfume and her hair was still damp from the shower. François kissed her on the mouth and gave me a pat on the back. They spoke in loud voices. I wondered how they managed to be so bright eyed that early in the morning. Our friend gave me his newspaper and asked for a cup of coffee in exchange. I confess to feeling quite relieved when the door finally closed behind them, and I was able to return to the bedroom. I threw the paper to one side and climbed back into bed. But I couldn't get back to sleep. I had the feeling of having a lot to do in a very short time. But in fact, all I had to do was to call Silvia and move in with her. That was the problem! There is nothing more exhausting than having to cut an interesting figure two days in a row. I wasn't calm, cool and collected like François. I could visualize Silvia stretching herself wearily, yawning, and fixing me with that look of despondent curiosity both teachers and women give you when they are waiting to be surprised. The next two days could turn into a nightmare. Still, I reflected, I shouldn't give up before starting. I had often overcome unexpected challenges through intuition and my peculiar ability for intellectual improvisation, which became more creative and devious, the stickier the situation. *I'll think of something* had always been my motto. So I decided to stop worrying. I got out of bed again, picked up the telephone, and called Silvia.

"Do you know what time it is?" she said, startled, when she heard my voice.

I had forgotten it was so early.

"I thought I'd bring you breakfast in bed," I blurted out, aware that when someone asks you a rhetorical question like what time it is, the best thing is an effective rejoinder. "François told me to take care of you."

My quick thinking had worked enviably well, even allowing me a malicious remark I would never have dared make had I had time to reflect. It was a rather tasteless aside, but tastelessness never harms the one who practices it. Silvia giggled sleepily and asked me to let her sleep a bit more. I wasn't feeling particularly proud of myself, but that didn't stop me from suffering a genuine attack of early-morning zeal. As I was alone, I sang the crudest ever version of the toast in *La Traviata* in the shower. I felt *smug,* which is possibly the ugliest, most categorical word in the dictionary. Smug and benevolent. Silvia wanted to sleep a bit longer and I wouldn't be the one to stand in her way. I sat down with my coffee and glanced through the newspaper. Shortly after, when I rose to get dressed, I discovered I couldn't remember a single news item I had read. That was a good sign. It meant my brain was busy concocting wonderful plans, which I would later suggest to Silvia without even realizing it. Why did so many fear their subconscious mind, when it was the only tool at their disposal to preserve a state of delicious indolence? What was wrong in allowing our brain the pleasure of saving our lives unbeknownst to us in the same way as our heart, kidneys, and, in fact, our entire body did? I left the house thinking that I would far rather regard my intellect as an attic filled with surprises than a storeroom I was obliged to keep tidy. And so I resolved to always obey my gut instinct.

I went to Esperanza's store and bought everything in sight. Jam, mini-toasts, smoked salmon, sweet rolls, tropical fruit juice... The problem with the subconscious mind is that it leaves the tiresome formality of earning money up to us. At the florist I chose an extremely elegant bouquet of pale orange roses. When I reached Silvia's place, I had the uncomfortable feeling I looked like the delivery boy. She still wasn't up. She let me in then went straight back to bed without pausing to greet me. I caught a glimpse of her naked body scurrying toward the bedroom. I had never seen anyone run with such wonderful gracelessness. I went straight to the kitchen. I laid the food out on two separate trays and arranged the roses in a porcelain vase. I could have done with a couple of servants to help carry everything into Silvia's room. As I didn't have any, I went back and forth a few times while she watched me with an amused expression. For the moment, I hadn't failed to live up to her expectations. I lay down on the bed beside her. Silvia sat up like a sick schoolgirl and greedily devoured the evil Esperanza's delicacies. Then (after I had done as she asked and taken away the trays and placed the roses where she could see them) she flung her arms around my neck and asked me to make love to her.

Silvia had the rare virtue of behaving exactly the same whether she was your friend or your lover. Let me explain. There was no intrinsic difference between making love to her and watching her eat an ice cream. And by this I don't mean that the desire to possess her was satisfied simply by watching her. I mean you couldn't help but end up identifying with the ice cream, if only because Silvia enjoyed both equally as she did everything she got her hands on. She was the most easily satisfied person I had ever known, and that was part of her charm. And yet, oddly, by the same token, it seemed as if nothing (not you or the damned ice cream) was able to satisfy her completely. Unlike Irene, who would sink into a profound, post-coital lethargy, Silvia emerged from lovemaking like a lost child, instantly demanding some fresh form of entertainment. For the second time that day, I left everything to improvisation. The weather was cold but sunny. While Silvia was getting ready, I went out and came back with a rented car. We drove down the coast road to Vilassar. I knew a restaurant overlooking the Mediterranean, where the seafood was even better than in the Caribbean. Silvia sat with her knees resting against the dashboard, browsing through a magazine and humming to herself. She led such a charmed life that she hadn't even bothered to ask where I was taking her. She would have been happy. In the meantime, I looked at her out of the corner of my eye and wondered what the two of us were doing sitting in that car, each immersed in our own thoughts, doing our best to kill time just like any other couple of secret adulterers. No one seeing us would have thought any different, and that made me feel much more of a heel than during our trysts in the Casita Blanca. I could sleep with a friend's wife and believe I was irresistibly attracted to her. But to go everywhere with her (encroaching, as it were, on normal life) felt more like an unjustifiable identity theft. Needless to say, none of this bothered Silvia in the slightest. She would have been incapable of understanding had I tried to explain it to her. When she spoke to me she showed the same spontaneity and familiarity as when addressing François. At one point, she even rested a hand on my leg for a while. I felt like a rat. The woman by my side wasn't a lover to whom I was tethered by chains of boundless lust; she was a beautiful wife about to enjoy a pleasant day by the sea! I was surprised Silvia didn't feel the same way. Although, as I mentioned before, she suffered from a kind of fatalistic masochism, that made her submissive in spite of her aloof nature. In addition, women have a definite tendency to stick by their decisions, and that means they are sometimes condemned to put up with men who are wracked with self-doubt. In short, you could say that I stayed with Silvia because I felt powerless to do anything else, and that Silvia stayed with me because she was faithful even to her own infidelity.

We sat next to a picture window and ate our meal in serene silence. Silvia narrowed her eyes in order to enjoy the sun on her face. The fact was we felt at ease without any need to get into bed. It was dreadful, terrible. I could no longer deceive myself. We were a couple of despicable wretches enjoying a few pleasant days together without risking anything at all. How could we grow tired of each other's company when we were protected by several years of friendship, when we had been occasional lovers all winter knowing we didn't want to take things further? Ours was a kind of free-lance marriage, a secret agreement enforced only when no one could see us, and only because it was what we both wanted at that moment: a classic case of practical passion. It was absurd for me to carry on feeling wretched about it when I had no intention whatsoever of doing anything to avoid it. So I gave myself over to the joys of contemplating Sylvia, which had always been one of my favorite occupations. Nor was it so reprehensible that a long-time admirer such as I should end up wanting to paw the object of his devotion. On the contrary, I should consider myself lucky to have found a discreet way of doing so. We chronic fence sitters have strange ways of ending up being at peace with ourselves. That was to be my last inner defense, because from then on I felt completely justified. With the satisfaction of the rascal who writes obscenities in a public toilet because he knows no one can see him, I grasped Silvia's chin, told her she was the most beautiful woman I had ever seen, and kissed her on the lips.

I knocked over her glass of wine. For some unknown reason that made her burst out laughing. I suppose it was because she felt at ease and was in a good mood. The waiter covered the stain with a cloth and brought us two coffees. Then Silvia stretched (yes, finally she did) and gave me an enquiring look. Naturally, we weren't going to sit there forever. I had been so wrapped up in my reflections that my improvisation skills were languishing in some inaccessible part of my brain. I took too long to come up with a suggestion. Silvia looked at me mischievously and graciously granted me a clue.

"I feel like having a siesta, but I don't want to go back to Barcelona."

Why hadn't I thought of that? Couples who devote themselves entirely to pleasure and are momentarily free from all obligations and the need to keep up any pretense, spend all their time searching for good restaurants and out of the way rooms. We had to find a hotel nearby. The one François had recommended to us came to mind. I felt a bit of a swine taking Silvia to the same place he had taken his young girlfriend, but my idea contained an element of hidden revenge. I thought it might appeal to Silvia. Besides (although I no longer believed one jot in my proverbial excuse), this was surely a way of tempting fate. We knew it was a place where the flame of passion might be extinguished.

"We're not far from Caldetas," I said to her. "We could go for a walk on the beach and try some Catalan sausage with prawns."

Silvia agreed, she always agreed. Back in the car, I remembered the thing that had really made François despair was precisely his lover's unflappable calm. But there was a huge difference. I had come to an agreement with myself that allowed me not to suffer because of things I would no longer be able to do. In fact, what I was doing then was so outrageous I didn't think it could go much further.

The hotel was the perfect place to hide away from the world. It had large, empty, covered terraces from which to view the sea. Being off-season, the hotel had an air of neglect. The halls were covered in a thin layer of dust and the sound of footsteps echoed as in a deserted palace. The furniture possessed that strange dignity of objects that have aged without ever having been grand. The whole place had an air of hibernation, including the receptionist. The buttons on his jacket must have been gold-plated in some splendid bygone age. We peered into the dining room. It was the only part of the hotel that showed any sign of life. The rest of the building faced the beach, but this room had its own entrance, which gave on to the square, and from there you could see the railroad station. It was the ideal place to shut yourself away with a woman and devote yourself entirely to discovering her. In any case, I thought, all that peace and quiet must have bored François' young friend stiff. François knew what he was doing, and had obviously taken her there in order to lose her without having to take the decision himself. He had found a way to be left high and dry.

The room they gave us was bathed in a pale, wintry light. The sun was weakening. They had turned the heating on, but it hadn't warmed the air yet. Silvia shivered. She rubbed her arms then placed her hands on the radiator. She gave me a rather puzzled look, as though (casually) wondering what I was doing there next to her. That was normal. She was tired. And yet that look was enough to remind me how fragile our union was. Although, miraculously, everything was going exactly the way I would have wanted, it still bothered me to discover that there weren't going to be any surprises. I would have been horrified if Silvia had given me an adoring look I would have been incapable of restraining. I would have thought (no doubt with indignation) that because of her naivety our pact had been broken. But at the same time, I couldn't help feeling a terrible yearning: for what might have been, somewhere else, had things only been different.

Those accursed doubts again. Would a provisional agreement suffice to cover the intense relationship we were bound to have? Was there any point in becoming someone's lover only if the possibility of love had been ruled out from the very beginning? Had we really become so damn *sensible*? I didn't want to give it any more thought, but it was too late to stop myself from feeling overwhelmed with melancholy. I gazed out of the window at the deserted beach. Behind me, Silvia undressed and climbed into bed. She wasn't expecting me to do the same. She was sleepy. In fact, my presence in the room was superfluous, because at that moment not only were we no longer lovers but also we had decided not to be anything else. All I could do was to wait until she woke up.

I spent almost two hours contemplating the empty beach through the window. That hiatus helped me realize I had had a moment of dangerous weakness. A lover is someone who comes in and out of your life without having to give any explanations, especially not of a sentimental nature. Besides, I had already decided I wouldn't allow myself any fresh indecisions. It was dark when Silvia called out to me softly. I turned toward her. Her eyes were shining in the half-light. I climbed into bed beside her. It took very little effort for Silvia to dispel my doubts, she did it without realizing. I fondled her breasts and slid my hand along the curve of her hip. The inside of her thighs was moist. Surrendering unreservedly to that scarcely fatal attraction, I became aroused by the thought that I had no right to touch her that way, that once again Silvia was making a gift of herself to me. My head filled with lascivious thoughts and Silvia responded with playful complicity. To my slight surprise, we enjoyed our most intense and drawn-out coupling. Our tongues ached from licking each other so much. There was such a strong smell of sex around us that, in a moment of delirium, I imagined the stagnant air in the room condensing and falling on us as aphrodisiac rain. We had to take a shower to freshen up before going out for a walk. That was the first time Silvia had allowed herself to be carried away by a passion that didn't seem accidental. Emerging from the bathroom she sat on the bed and gave a sigh. She was experiencing conflicting feelings, but for her they were all pleasurable and hardly conclusive. Finally, she gave a shrug and got dressed in her usual ungainly way. She didn't put on any underwear. Gazing at me tenderly, her arms around my neck, she said she wanted me to touch her constantly wherever we went. I kissed her with such fervor that for a moment I was afraid we were not respecting our agreement. The truth was we had finally let go without straying beyond the very narrow limits of our territory. I was confused by my own limitless capacities. I had left my accursed doubts behind. I could have a lover, and I could share moments of such intense passion with her that it no longer mattered whether I then lost her forever. After that, who cared what happened next? We kissed again, and resolved (in whispers, as though being alone weren't enough, and we wanted to wrap ourselves in each other) to leave the windows closed so that our smell would impregnate the room and still be there when we got back. We opened the door, I put my arm around Silvia's waist and we stepped into the corridor. At that same moment, another door opened and Irene and François appeared, they too with their arms around each other.

All four of us instinctively let go of each other with incredible speed. But after our belated attempt not to be where we were, we were incapable of making any other movement. A laugh (from François I think) had crystallized in the air. We all stood motionless, looking at one another with a surprise that far outstripped our ability to respond. Irene was the first to understand what was going on.

"This can't be happening," she murmured, as though refusing to believe her own eyes.

But her bewilderment was momentary. She leapt at me, pushing me violently so that I fell back against the wall.

"You son of a bitch! Silvia was my friend! My friend!"

This made my lover react, and she tried to intervene.

"Irene," she said, taking a step toward her.

"Don't you dare say a word. Shut up!"

As though her command weren't enough, she looked daggers at Silvia, who stopped dead in her tracks. Then, turning to me once more, she inhaled, steadying herself to hurl one final insult.

"Go to hell, you bastard."

She turned round and started marching down the corridor, but came back straightaway. She asked François for some money. François, who hadn't moved an inch, handed her a few banknotes. He caught her arm, and said he would go with her. Irene wheeled round angrily and went off on her own toward the stairs. I was dumbfounded. Irene certainly had quicker reactions than me, but she was also far better at scorn. I had just as much right as she did to be angry. And yet, Irene hadn't given me a chance. What made it worse, it had never occurred to me she might be having an affair with François, but I wasn't annoyed at all, on the contrary, I started torturing myself thinking how much she must be suffering. It wasn't my innate goodness that made me suffer on her behalf. It was just that I knew how incredibly vulnerable she was. Only someone as fragile as Irene could allow herself the luxury of having such a subjective response, and moreover without losing her composure. Nobody is perfect. As someone who is permanently disillusioned, my idea of morality was so tenuous that I was prone to being as responsive as a wax dummy. While Irene, who had a limitless capacity for disillusionment, was able to forget her own guilt completely.

But I was in for another surprise. I was still leaning on the wall Irene had thrown me against. All I could think was that the whole thing was crazy, when I heard my lover's voice addressing François:

"You could have told me you were coming here."

"It's unbelievable," he replied. "Of all the *millions* of hotels in the world, you had to come to this one."

I was aware they didn't hide their infidelities from each other, but I never imagined their frankness could reach such extremes. I cringed as I recalled all the times François had clapped me on the back, my sly remarks and my pathetic belief that Silvia and I shared a secret no one else knew about.

"We should go," I heard François say.

Silvia gave me a peck on the cheek. He made a move toward me, but paused as though unsure what to do.

"I'm sorry," he said.

As they walked down the corridor I looked up at them. François had his arm around Silvia's shoulders. That marked the end of many things. I wondered if there would be anything left for me to start over with the next day. I waited for a few moments and then went downstairs to the dining room. I sat in a corner. A very fat woman walked over to me swinging her hips.

"Good evening, Montserrat," I said to her. "I'd like to try some of your Catalan sausage with prawns."

I spent the night there, although before going to sleep I opened the windows to air the room. I knew Irene well and I knew it was pointless to try to contact her while she was still angry. I didn't sleep a wink the whole night.

Predictably, each time I closed my eyes I found myself back in the hospital and the dead man's ghostly feet loomed, almost threateningly, as though about to trample on me. Day dawned so slowly I had the impression time had stopped, abandoning me in that hotel room. A dense cloud of silence enveloped me making me painfully aware of every sound I made. The hiss of air leaving my lungs, the clunk of the lighter as I placed it on the bedside table, the swish of sheets as I moved my legs. I had to clear my throat loudly to break that oppressive silence with a harsh sound. At that moment I was living in my own book, that book which was impossible to write, and which was suddenly beginning to close in on me, as though wanting to prove to me, once and for all, that a man who is born blind will never know what the world looks like even if he spends his entire life trying. When I finally managed to leave the room, I went down to the foyer to ask the receptionist for the bill.

"The other gentleman settled everything. You only owe me for the dinner."

It felt as if he had stabbed the very heart of my self-respect.

"Stop talking nonsense and tell me how much I owe you for the room. You can give him a refund when he comes back."

He looked at me doubtfully. I imagined he was not sure whether to do as I said or maintain the stubborn attitude of an unbribable employee. He must have decided he didn't want any trouble, because he shrugged his shoulders and sat down in order to make out the bill.

"This is a bit irregular," he murmured as he wrote. "It's the first time anything like this has happened to me."

He paused and gave me a solemn look.

"You know, people always hope someone else will pay the bill. When I tell them it has already been paid they're usually relieved."

"That gentleman stole his wife from me and caused me to lose mine, with whom incidentally he was having an affair," I replied, irritated.

The receptionist gave me a knowing look and carried on writing. I cursed myself for having blurted out my troubles to him, but I was tired of all that silence, and the endless dawn. I wanted someone to tell me I was in the right, or at least to show an iota of sympathy for my wretched situation. However, hotel receptionists aren't known for their boundless interest in their customers' personal lives, even in the rare event they pay their bill twice. He didn't speak to me again.

I drove to Barcelona in a state of complete confusion. I returned the rented car and hailed a cab. On the way home I tried to imagine a logical way of entering the house. It was very early. I could let myself be guided again by the art of improvisation and bring Irene breakfast in bed, just as I had with Silvia. A splendid breakfast and an enormous bouquet of roses. No, that would be folly. Irene was clearly going to be confrontational. At that moment she only wanted to unleash her anger on me, and everything concerning me. And besides, I planned to give as good as I got (I had every reason to), so the roses would end up strewn over the floor. Besides, if I bought them straightaway, I would have used up the trump card I might need the next day, when the faint possibility of things returning to normal would begin to emerge. I didn't have a lot of options. For the moment, all I could do was walk in ready for the firing squad, displaying that common sense that so unsettled her.

I opened the door with my heart in my mouth. The house was silent. I called Irene's name a few times but there was no reply. It was possible she hadn't slept there, but I found it difficult to imagine her asking anyone for help. Those who run to the aid of their friends are extremely independent when they themselves are facing a crisis. Irene would have had to come home because it was the only place she could be alone. Perhaps she was still asleep, though it seemed unlikely and even a bit insulting. That possibility gave me renewed strength. In spite of having also been caught red-handed, Irene had flown into a jealous rage before returning home to sleep peacefully, while I struggled with an attack of insomnia worthy of Scott Fitzgerald. I marched into the bedroom ready to take the initiative.

The bed was empty. It hadn't been slept in, but the wardrobe doors stood open and the overall chaos bore all the signs of a hasty departure. Irene had taken all her belongings, including the photograph of the little girl with the tortoise. I went back into the living room and flung myself onto the sofa. I was so stunned my only thought was that I was the victim of a woman suffering from the most ridiculous form of insanity. Wasn't she as guilty as I, and moreover in a perverse way, because she had made up a tall tale in order to go away with her lover? Why did she turn her formidable capacity for anger on me instead of venting it on herself? Why did everyone (including me) think Irene had such *integrity* when in fact she was just as self-centered as everyone else? Perhaps it was because of her exaggerated ability to suffer.

I sat up on the sofa with a start. I mustn't forget that like me Irene was full of contradictions, but she was also unbearably clear-headed. Perhaps she was not only angry with me but with herself (with both of us), and had decided that if we stayed together we were doomed to make each other suffer. I had always been terrified of Irene making important decisions, because she was capable of carrying them out. Her well-known integrity might mean losing her forever.

When Rosario arrived I hadn't moved from the sofa. I answered her greeting with a grunt. She brought me a cup of coffee and shut herself in the kitchen. After a while the telephone rang. I leapt at the receiver.

"I want to speak to Rosario," Irene said.

Her voice calmed me, although she sounded like an operator who is sick and tired of her job. Too perfect, too devoid of any emotional tie.

"We have to talk," I blurted out. "I've been awake all night thinking. I'm exhausted, but I want to see you."

"If you don't put Rosario on right now I'll hang up."

"All right, all right. Stay where you are."

I called Rosario. She appeared wiping her hands on her apron and raised her eyebrows as she took the receiver. She always did that when she had to pay attention to something. She nodded silently a few times. I could hear Irene's voice transformed into an unintelligible metallic buzz. Rosario gave a squeal of surprise. She looked at me in alarm, but Irene kept talking. She nodded a few more times. Then she put her hand over the mouthpiece.

"She's going to Nicaragua," she whispered.

I leapt in the air like a cat that has just received a hunter's bullet in its haunch. I snatched the phone from her.

"Irene, don't do anything foolish. Things are bad here, but the Caribbean dream is as unreal as utopias or beggars with millions in the bank. For us, the Caribbean is the same as Caltanissetta. They aren't real. Where are you?"

I heard a continuous bleep. Flat-lined cardiogram. She had hung up.

During the following weeks I would discover (continuing, incidentally, a rather Western tradition) something obvious I already knew: that silence was no more than an absence, and, therefore, regardless of how many sounds I enveloped myself in, if the ones I expected to hear weren't among them, it could become absolute. The faint clink of glass on glass as Irene, lost in thought, got ready in the bathroom; the pad of her footsteps coming down the corridor behind me; her tinkling laughter as she spoke on the phone, while I wondered, idly suspicious, with whom she was now sharing that bubble of fun-loving intimacy. During those weeks,

161

I would often wheel around, startled, not by a sudden sound, but by its absence, which was far more unnerving than the most distressing everyday noise. Few things affected me as much as suddenly hearing a sound that had never been there before, because it was the clearest indication that my brain cells were willing to believe in something that didn't exist. Madness roamed through me manifesting itself in its most elementary forms, throwing up fleeting mirages that dissolved the moment I started to believe they were real. One evening, while I was sitting by the fire, I became so intensely aware of Irene's hand on my shoulder that I could feel her body heat through my shirt. Momentarily beguiled, I brushed off my shoulder angrily, as if someone had emptied an ashtray on it. Many times I caught myself wanting to tell her something, and it was during those moments when I felt obliged to hold my tongue in order not to act like a madman (because my good judgment however weakened, was a witness with a great flair for analyzing things immediately), when I was overwhelmingly tempted to conclude that we were alone in this world, and that talking, making love or living with another human being were all sophisticated ways of not saying anything to each other, because there was nothing to say.

None of that, however, would prevent me from trying to stop Irene. Unfortunately, she demonstrated a rare gift for making herself scarce while showing up everywhere. She had vanished, but only as far as I was concerned. In the days prior to her departure she had several conversations with Rosario. In fact, she continued running the household from her absurd exile in no-man's land. Once Rosario turned up and cleaned the windows, because, she said, Irene had asked her to. Another time, she made a dish obeying the whims of the eternally absent one, who wasn't going to eat it. And so our domestic goddess was able to carry on her usual activities as though nothing had happened, but for me it became the worst kind of torture. Irene (I shall always begrudge slightly her subtle ability to crucify me even at the expense of tormenting herself, the worst form of twisted egotism) managed to evaporate with an intensity she had perhaps never bothered to have. I searched for her in vain all over Barcelona. Cities seem so small when it comes to chance encounters, which happen constantly as if we were all out there stumbling over one another, but they become too big as soon as we want to find something specific. Such as a woman who has been doubly hurt by a mutual betrayal and has decided to become invisible only to the eyes of the one most desperate to see her.

I was never one to get to the bottom of things. Even close to suicide I would have lacked the conviction to do so, which was a manner of speaking because I also lacked the conviction to be truly suicidal. I had always considered that in order to take your own life respectably you had to be truly desperate. And, in my view, despair was the most mediocre way one could respond to the daily ordeal of getting out of bed in the morning and pressing on for no reason. I had the advantage of not liking having anyone waiting for me anywhere. That meant I was in the habit of getting out of bed with

163

almost cheerful indifference, convinced, above all, that I wasn't going anywhere, nor was I going to throw myself off the balcony like Olga's husband, which would have been nonsensical living on the mezzanine. I was never one to investigate things too deeply, and yet Irene's disappearance (exacerbated by the threat of her imminent flight to the Caribbean, a place which no doubt didn't exist) aroused the private investigator in me. At last I had discovered something that made getting out of the house worthwhile.

I started off by arranging to meet Olga at a café in the city center. She came with her sons, who had left their childhood behind somewhere in Paris. They no longer chased each other round the tables. They sat with us and succumbed to tedium with that passionate indolence only teenagers can muster. They reminded me of the time, long ago, when I too felt an infinite longing for what the future had in store. But if life consisted of running a race against longing, I had to admit I had overtaken it at a hotel in Caldetas and left it all behind me, further and further in the past, and I found myself firmly ensconced in a time when you simply try to salvage what you can of the things you have lost along the way.

Olga took my hands in hers and asked me several times how I was feeling. I was sure she knew where Irene was hiding. Since she was looking at me with genuine concern, I allowed my face to take on a pained expression. When you can hardly bear your own state of mind, you are particularly open to improvising, especially when what is required is a bit of tragedy.

My tear ducts started tingling, and I could no longer contain myself. The boys clicked their tongues, clearly bothered by the scene unfolding in front of them. But Olga leaned forward and kissed my hands. When someone kisses your hands (unlike other seemingly more passionate kisses) they are willing to do anything for you.

"Order me another beer and tell me where Irene is."

Much to my astonishment, and (I must confess) my restrained indignation, Olga shook her head. She called the waiter over with a soft movement of her delicate, swan-like neck. When she had given the order, she patted my forearm good-naturedly.

"Irene doesn't want you to follow her or try to dissuade her. All she wants is for you to immerse yourself fully in your book."

The tears dried on my cheeks. To what book was that idiot Irene referring? Our history of silence? Did she expect me to shut myself away again in that dank cell with Saint Nepomuk while she abandoned herself to effortless Caribbean orgies? Did she think I was going to spend bitter nights in the company of Fitzgerald while she drank rum and went skinny-dipping on the beach? Did she have the gall to abandon our project and submerge herself, at least where I was concerned, in the most absolute silence so that I would spell out for her in a lengthy treatise how alone I felt? No way. Olga had to tell me where Irene was hiding. She owed me that much. I had stood by and aided her in that sort of second-degree murder, the desperate shove (for want of a better expression) that had allowed her depressed husband to leap from the window and free her from his presence forever.

"You owe me a favor," I told her. "I want you to return it *now.*"

Olga gave me an inscrutable smile. She knew what I was talking about.

"That's exactly what I'm doing this very minute, even if right now you don't want to know. Irene is running wild again. It's best to steer clear of her. If you want to catch her, you'll have to start over."

That was the last thing I wanted to hear. Start anew. Go back to the beginning when I had already gone beyond longing and all I wanted was to glue the broken pieces back together. I looked at Olga angrily and she responded with an even broader grin.

"Do you want me to let you into a secret?" she said in her most enigmatic voice. "You have to make a woman fall in love with you more than once in a lifetime."

One morning I disobeyed Irene's wishes. I did so more in order to be annoying than in the hope of gaining anything from my search. My beloved had an almost fatalistic respect for destiny, though she saw no problem in correcting it with her most irrefutable decisions. The somewhat ironical consequence of this was that she obeyed her own dictates with the same resignation as she did those imposed on her by the order of things, to the point where she forgot which had been decreed by her and which by the wheel of fortune. That made me furious, because Irene ended up yielding to herself, which was a glaring contradiction. So I resolved to disobey her, if only in order to tell her she alone was responsible for her running away, and consequently I refused to buy in to any theatrical gestures about succumbing to a higher power. I was sure the idea of leaving me and going to the Caribbean hadn't formed in Irene's head all of a sudden in that hotel corridor where we discovered we were being unfaithful to each other, but had been slowly incubating since that fated evening beside the fireplace when she started dreaming of distant drums and cockatoos' cries. From then on she must have always had the lure of a mango levitating in front of her eyes.

I knew that Clara and Johnny were staying at a two-star hotel in Plaza Real with a pompous name that reflected their situation perfectly: *Hotel Ambos Mundos* (Both Worlds). I turned up there before noon and asked for them at reception. Clara had gone out, but Johnny was in their room. I knew Irene wouldn't be hiding out there, but I asked for her too. The receptionist shook her head, and began looking at me suspiciously. I asked him to tell Johnny I was there. While I was waiting I stared at the square through the glass door. It was cold and overcast, yet immigrants and pensioners filled the benches. A patrol car was driving leisurely past the palm trees. I had the impression that (like the jellyfish in our aborted book) it was a sightless monster eagerly awaiting the slightest movement in order to locate its next victim. As it rolled, very slowly, past the hotel, I stayed still like a tiny, intuitive pulsating sheet. The story had to have some use, after all. Johnny's voice jolted me out of my cover. He lunged at me, grabbing my shoulders and shaking me. It seemed incredible that he was so happy to see me and that my lack of response didn't faze him. I have always had a tendency to pride myself on my natural reserve. But that morning, for an instant, I felt like a rag doll in the hands of a black giant. I was even surprised that with all the ruckus the patrol car didn't come crashing in through the glass door.

"Where've you been hiding, brother? It's great to see you! Let's have a beer to celebrate! There's a bar near here where the grilled sardines are to die for. I should know, man, I'm the King of Sardines!"

Why was it that, despite his boundless enthusiasm, Johnny always conveyed to me an underlying message of repressed sadness? Why did people who were always cheerful give me that impression? As we crossed the square (thank goodness the hungry jellyfish had disappeared) it occurred to me that melancholy sometimes revealed itself in the most surprising ways.

We leaned our elbows on the bar of a run down tavern and two glasses of frothy beer were placed in front of us. A woman reading a newspaper grudgingly stood up and went to grill the sardines. Johnny was eager to drink to his fishing boats that were in Galicia awaiting the order to set sail.

"We're taking them through the Panama Canal," he said, "and from there non-stop to Corinto. I wanted to go with the boats, but Clara is too afraid. Can you believe it? We'll fly out and wait for them at the dockside, our hearts in our mouths."

If I didn't do something, Johnny would keep on talking in order to avoid my question. And so I blurted it out:

"I need to see Irene. I want you to tell me where she's hiding."

"Of course you do," he said jovially but without smiling. "I can't tell you that, brother. Your chick would kill me. Of course she would."

I remained silent in a way that must have disconcerted him. He sipped his beer and looked at me with a hangdog expression, although his smile was back. I realized I couldn't persuade him to reveal the information. He had promised not to tell me and he was a man of his word. It occurred to me (by then I no longer cared whether I was being unfair or not) that our friends had all rallied round Irene and were obeying her without worrying that she might be doing something desperate. Perhaps they even thought she would be better off away from someone like me.

"Listen, man, I'll tell you what I can do," Johnny declared, crestfallen but still jubilant. "I'll give you my address in Managua, that way, if you like, I can act as a go-between. Things here will look different from over there."

He asked for a pen and scribbled his address on a paper napkin. He held out his gigantic hand. I stuffed the napkin into my pocket with the same indifference I showed when people offered me fliers in the street. I wished him the best of luck with his fishing boats, and left the bar without turning to wave him a last goodbye.

Out in the street I started wandering aimlessly. How could Irene disappear in a place as small as Barcelona, where, on top of everything, we knew so many people? It seemed impossible that in the end no one was willing to take my side. It seemed even less possible that, my friends having failed me, I couldn't at least count on a chance encounter or a happy coincidence. Suddenly, I had a flash of inspiration. Irene could change all her habits except those related to her work. She could even leave me and decide that I should finish (or start) our book by myself, but she would still have to keep going to the library. The big, old building was tucked down a side street not far from where I was. I stepped out onto the Ramblas and headed up Calle del Carmen. A fine rain had begun to fall, scattering the passers-by. I entered the Gothic cloister, where a few students were huddled beneath the arcades. This was Irene's true territory, the only place she would be faithful to. I walked through the cloister breathing in the scent of my beloved that seemed to pervade the entire compound. I climbed the stairs sensing her close, so sure of finding her that it wouldn't have surprised me to see her replicated in every corner of that place imbued with her presence. I walked through the computer room searching for her among the curved backs of the women who were engrossed in their computer screens. I went in to the reading room. The spacious tables were occupied by a studious crowd that seemed to be dozing off beneath the dim lights. Next to a counter piled high with books, a mild-mannered matron handled each volume with great care, as if it were made from some highly explosive material. A man in a grey coverall emerged from a side door pushing a rubber wheeled trolley. He approached the counter with the slowness of a judicious philosopher who has decided never to arrive at his destination. In that high-ceilinged room, with cross beams like in a church, the silence amplified until it became a muffled reverberation of echoes. I glanced toward Irene's usual place, but she wasn't there. I moved along the passageway sniffing her scent, which was perhaps too overpowering to be real. I searched in vain for the curve of her neck among the heads tilted over the open volumes. Finally, I picked out a reference book at random and sat down among the other readers. There was as much stillness (as much hushed, secret activity) as in an opium den. Perhaps that atmosphere of fervent concentration got the better of me, or perhaps the madness roaming through me found a foothold, but I looked at the door hoping to see Irene walk in and then I heard it. I distinctly heard the sound of books murmuring to each other, exchanging hidden confidences, secrets and revelations, in that maze of permanently dusty shelves, and I understood what Irene was searching for when she shut herself away in there: something more than simple information, something more than answers to the questions she might be able to ask, something that could doubtless not be uttered or written down and yet which existed within those walls, alive, palpable, mingled with the scent of my beloved, something so powerful that one could feed off it without worrying whether it was a harmless lie (another mirage of clear water) or a poison it would have been better never to have tried. And I knew that I wanted to sink with Irene into that bottomless pool, into that murmur of voices hushed for eternity, into that forever ineffable silence so intense that it had the power to dissolve all absences, the strongest anxiety, even life itself, and was so beautiful and so terrible that at its core one ceased to be wretched and betrayals were true betrayals, love became sublime and death was transformed into something magnificent that rejected mediocre souls. And all thanks to the enormous simulacrum called literature, perhaps the only honest activity of a species accustomed to deception. Life, which I habitually regarded as a tedious outing, was for Irene an open wound through which that splendor, doubtless an illusion, entered her body. I realized that, behind her gray eyes, Irene concealed that inconsequential secret, and finally I realized that no matter how many plates we smashed, I couldn't live without her, without contemplating in her the obscured glimmer, the warm promise of that truly useless treasure.

Everyone was very worried about me. Irene was already in Nicaragua. She had gone without leaving me a goodbye note. Johnny's boats were sailing through Caribbean waters on their way to Panama, crewed by black men proud of their good fortune. What did they care if the vessels were second-hand and a lunatic businessman from Barcelona was bankrolling their adventure? At last they were bringing something positive from the Old World. Clara and Johnny (and perhaps Irene) were eagerly waiting for them their hearts in their mouths at the port of Corinto.

Olga arranged a dinner party at Amador's to cheer me up. I took two bottles of Rioja and downed a whole one myself before sitting down to eat. Natalia's arrival may have changed little in that house where a real geisha would have refused to set foot, but Amador was almost unrecognizable. He didn't sigh as exquisitely as before. He gave himself airs even if the topic of conversation was stamp collecting. But, on the subject of women (or love in the broadest sense, including brutal, raw sex) he practically swooned under the weight of all his wisdom. Whenever Natalia walked past him he would pat her bottom (imitating François, perhaps) and she would give him a sideways glance, unable to comprehend what was wrong with him. Then Amador would give a little giggle that set my teeth on edge.

They all looked at me oddly. Olga kept grabbing my arm with an anxious fervor. Her small, white hands clung to me like limpets, and, having exhausted her ability to ask me how I was, she was content to observe me with helpless unease. There is little friends can do for each other, except perhaps if the one in need uses the other the way she had used me. Olga was willing, at that moment, to let me manipulate her, however clumsily, if it would be of any help. But she was incapable of understanding that I was far more skeptical than her, and, accustomed as I was to having things presented to me on a plate or calmly accepting their loss, it would be difficult for me to come up with a ploy to achieve something or win it back. I had been around long enough to consider that life had already surprised me too often for me to believe it wouldn't continue to do so however much I tried to prevent it, which was another way of losing the battle.

"You're a good friend," I said, impatiently, forcing her to let go of my arm so that I could disengage slightly and pour myself another glass of wine.

I wished I hadn't gone to the dinner party. Amador had shut himself away in the kitchen while Natalia was setting the table. Olga amused herself by flicking through his LPs, which she must have known by heart, as they were always the same old ones. Leaning against the wall, I remembered the evenings when Irene and I, and Silvia and François, would try out new restaurants where we could repeat ad infinitum our furtive exchange of glances, I also remembered, in that apartment frozen in time, my lover sitting across the room defying me with her haughtiest gaze, savoring the perverse idea of fearing me, while Irene and François mapped out next to the cocktail bar the secret pathways that would allow the two of them to be alone, perhaps a trip to Madrid in the wrong direction. And it struck me how naïve Irene and I had been not to realize what was going on, how absorbed in our own mischief and therefore blind to the fact that our respective lovers were far more sophisticated and honest, and that they said nothing to us because (as furtive presences in our lives) they couldn't reveal the true nature of the game. Irene must have been tearing her hair out, not so much because she realized she was both betrayer and betrayed, but because she had been unaware of a perversion far more comprehensive in scope than her own. We had both committed the unpardonable sin of pride. The outcome could scarcely be more pathetic. Irene was so crazy she at least had the possibility of abandoning herself to the Caribbean dream. Life would become far more tedious for me from then on.

Once we were sitting round the table, Amador began boasting tastelessly about his love life. I understood his wanting to take revenge for all the years of unhappiness, but I couldn't stomach him doing so at my expense. He looked at Olga and then at me, shaking his head, with a half-smile, insinuating that, unlike him, we were incapable of finding a stable but passionate relationship. At any moment he would start offering us advice. Natalia no longer turned pale in our company. She had even become an unbearable chatterbox, capable, in a few minutes, of recommending several films we *had to* see, a handful of books we couldn't possibly not have read, and even a relaxation method for before going to bed. She gazed at me intently and said that Amador had told her I was taking too many Valium, and that's why I *had* to try her method. The vast majority of shy people should remain so forever. Olga, in contrast, kept quiet. She ate in silence, her eyes fixed on her plate. Her natural eloquence seemed to have been snuffed out, or perhaps she was saving it up for new, more entertaining company. That was all that was left of my life with Irene, the remains of a world I had come to find oppressive but which was turning out to be as insubstantial as a bad stage play where the actors no longer take their roles seriously. I for one felt I had played myself for long enough.

"Excuse me," I said, rising. "I have to go to the bathroom."

I left the dining room, took my coat off the coat rack and very quietly opened the front door. I left it ajar so that they wouldn't hear the lock clicking shut.

I had sat up all night in the living room staring at the bamboo plants in the moonlight. Rosario cast me a worried glance when she arrived, though she had grown used to finding me there in the morning. She lit the fire and covered me with a blanket. I thought I was destined to always end up being looked after by a nurse. The idea struck me as rather outlandish. The cold winter sun filtered through the windows making me squint. I didn't even feel truly depressed. Rosario brought me a cup of coffee and stood watching me, her hands folded over her stomach. I had been mulling obsessively over Olga's remark for several hours.

"Rosario," I said, "do you think a man has to make a woman fall in love with him more than once in a lifetime?"

She unfolded her arms with a joyous expression, as if I had inadvertently asked her the only question to which she knew the answer.

"Yes, many, many times. My husband brought me here from Huelva nearly ten years ago and has taken me for granted ever since, the fool. To be honest, sometimes I feel like making him think I don't love him anymore, just to bring him down a peg or two. Women are very simple. All we want is for everything to go on being *important*."

It bothered me slightly that the final decision should rest with passive types like me or Rosario's poor husband, when there were so many dynamic people in the world. Clearly, that man was content to go on reaping the rewards of a moonlit night in an Andalusian doorway, unaware that he was expected every so often to revive his ability to shake up other people's lives.

I felt around for my sunglasses on the sofa. Of course, they weren't there. Despite the exhaustion I felt simply thinking about what Rosario had said to me, I had to admit I agreed with her. Nothing is as disappointing to others as only being brilliant once in your life. And so, prey to nostalgia, I was forced to make an effort and I already knew what that would be. If Irene wanted a dramatic gesture, I would pay the most flamboyant homage I could think of to our (for various reasons) failed relationship. I had on my side our book about silence. Although it had also fallen by the wayside, it had provided us with a secret code which I could use to show her I had finally understood what she was looking for in the library, what she was looking for in my arms and in the arms of others, what she had hoped to find in our book, and above all what consumed her when she was quiet. I didn't have to show her that she was important to me (a fact that would have left her cold, because if Irene was skeptical about anything it was her own importance), but rather that I was important to her.

The solution lay in an image, which might be rather irksome for a writer. But I have never been all that passionate about my profession. I threw off the blanket and abandoned my prolonged retreat on the sofa. I rummaged through the drawers in search of my Polaroid. It was loaded. I handed it to Rosario and, seizing her by the shoulders, placed her with her back to the bookcase. I stood in front of the wall opposite. Rosario, somewhat bewildered, looked warily at the camera. She raised her eyebrows very high when I spoke.

"All you have to do is press the button on the top. The camera will do the rest. I'm going to scream very loud, so don't be alarmed. When my face looks most distorted take my picture."

I clenched my fists and began screaming at the top of my voice. Rosario gazed at me with astonishment, but then raised the camera to her eyes. After shifting her weight from one leg to the other trying desperately to fit me in the frame, she finally took the snapshot just as I was about to die from asphyxia. The Polaroid made a buzzing sound and the photo slid out between her fingers. I took it from her before she could leave her fingerprints all over it. I put it in my pocket as I hurried off to search in my coat pocket for Johnny's napkin. There it was, crumpled but legible. I copied out the address on an envelope. Only then I went ahead and dared look at the photo. The image still wasn't fully exposed, but I could say unequivocally that it was the best picture anyone had ever taken of me. There was no doubt, that was me. Only Irene was capable of seeing that, and of seeing that she was the only one who knew what it meant. Love always ends up being a mysterious language only two people can decipher. I gave a triumphant cry. Rosario was still standing motionless beside the bookcase holding the camera, a look of horror on her face as if she had just shot me in the head at my request. I told her she had created a work of art. I really meant it. I put the photograph in the envelope and made my way to the door in order to post it. Stepping into the hallway I bumped straight into my neighbor. Alerted by my prolonged howls (gloriously domestic) she had come to my rescue brandishing a saw. Unlike my neighbor, Irene would never hear my magnificent lament. She would have to be content to *see it*.

Everything was ready. However, I had been invited to one final social event I didn't want to wriggle out of. If the encounter in Caldetas had demolished my relationship with Irene, it had also encouraged Silvia and François to move in together. As if that weren't enough (and with the additional pressure from their wealthy families, who used the inheritance question to make their case) they decided to marry in a civil ceremony one morning, just as spring made a surprise appearance with a freak heat wave. It seemed incredible that things always turned out so well for them.

   I went with Olga, who came to pick me up, delighted to be able to experience some good news at first hand. We all knew that Silvia and François were the only people capable of brightening up our lives. We couldn't imagine who had made this world, but we were convinced they had done so on the assumption that we were all like them. At the registry office, my companion, deeply moved, slipped her arm through mine while I

179

gave myself over completely to admiring Silvia. She looked stunning in a casual, scarlet raw silk suit, and so at ease in that dingy place, as if she could see wonders there we others had missed. I couldn't help but feel proud of her. Had I been able, I would have confided to the other guests that this exceptional bride had been my lover. I have to confess that even I was slightly moved when they kissed each other at the end of the ceremony. My back still tingled from the friendly pat François had given me after he spotted me among the people who had come to witness his and Silvia's decision to renounce the daily repetition of their first encounter in Paris. I wasn't exactly the right person to reproach them for it. Sometimes I think the only reason that wedding took place was so that everything could go back to normal. It was a little late for great declarations of friendship, but a lot of things had happened and we were in danger of losing our bearings, each in our own way. The ceremony turned out (as usual) to be a pact of non-aggression between all parties, a bit like an artificial Christmas. Even Amador and Natalia (whom I hadn't seen since I walked out on them, and who, according to Olga, had taken the *difficult but irrevocable decision to detest me*) came over to say hello like a couple of old friends. A huge banquet was held at an expensive restaurant, the last one we were to try out together, although instead of Irene there were over two hundred people with us. Silvia, and sometimes François, cast me knowing glances tinged with guilt through the throng of diners. I blew them heartfelt kisses, and raised my glass so many times I seemed to have become maudlin from the wine. The truth was I felt like a Parisian florist obliged to travel far from home and to sit among strangers. I kept my composure fairly well during the meal, but when the band started playing a bolero I thought I wouldn't be able to bear all that melancholy. I gave Olga a kiss and made my way over to the newlyweds' table. A few tiresome guests were calling the couple onto the dance floor, but they came toward me. At that moment we ceased to hear the din of the party. As if we had been granted a few quiet moments in which to say goodbye, the only sound echoing in our ears as we approached each other was our breathing. We inhaled the same air, the same yearning for a time that had been uniquely ours, and which, in spite of everything, still was. The ever-unruly Silvia hurled herself into my arms and clasped me round the neck. It was the last time I trembled at the touch of her body.

"Tell me you don't regret it," she whispered urgently, and, as always, playfully. "I'll die if you don't."

I didn't need to lie in order to tell her what she wanted to hear. Thanks to all that had happened, I too was ready be surprised by the future, and I had even more ways and means than they did. I had that crazy Irene who was running around on the other side of the world. François hesitated for a moment. He must have thought I was only there out of loyalty to his wife. But I hugged him. Once again, without having to lie, I told him that he was my only friend. My words moved him. With his usual enthusiasm, he hugged me back so hard he nearly cracked a couple of my ribs. It was time for me to leave. I turned around and the din of the party took center stage once more. As I walked toward the exit, I saw Silvia and François, still slightly dazed, being dragged on to the dance floor to start the dancing. I stepped outside thinking I had rather a lot to do and not much time to do it in. My plane was leaving early next morning.

Managua airport consisted of a single runway and a concrete building that looked more like a prison. From the air I had noticed the sparse vegetation surrounding the city. I had also heard that they were expecting an earthquake. The landscape was dotted with small grey buildings, and a few beat-up trucks threw up clouds of dust along the highways. The plane landed in that pathetic paradise with such a thud that I thought I might die without ever knowing whether Irene had come to meet me. The idea that she hadn't come terrified me to the point where I thought it would be a relief not to know. When I stepped onto the runway I was sure my legs were going to give way. I hadn't had the guts to tell Irene I was going there to join her, and I desperately hoped that Olga (the only one who knew about what our illustrious beggar had called my *Japanese decision*) had fulfilled her role of devoted confidante. I walked toward the terminal breathing in anxiously that heady atmosphere, saturated with smells that could intoxicate someone far more confident than I. It wasn't hot, but I was sweating so much my shirt was soaked through. I almost went back to the plane to ask if they would let me on again. As I reached the terminal, I stopped, horrified, in my tracks. Someone behind gave me a shove and I stumbled inside. Behind a large pane of glass, a group of people were waiting for us to arrive. I ran my eyes over them with such anguish that I didn't see anything. I ran my hands over my face and looked again.

There were her smiling gray eyes, floating amidst the reflections on the glass. Her hair was longer, her skin was incredibly brown and she was wearing a dress I hadn't seen before. But it was the same Irene who looked for me in her sleep without knowing it, the same Irene who feared for her friends and who shut herself away in a distant library to listen to the secret conversations books have with each other, that pointless mystery it had taken me so long to discover. I handed over my passport with the impatience of a businessman exasperated by the officialdom of Third World countries. When they let me through, I ran toward Irene and kissed her with an abandon that was decidedly Parisian.

"Promise me you won't run away again," I said. "I want to be with you."

Irene chuckled. We held each other as if we were afraid that any moment a strange force might come between us.

"I want to be with you, too," she replied. "Now you've said it. You can be quiet for a few more years."

A large black lady had come to a halt right beside us and was staring at us with an idiotically happy grin.

"Go away, please," I implored.

She nodded, but kept the same expression and didn't move an inch. Irene slipped her arm around my waist and guided me toward the exit. I had such palpitations

I thought I was going to have a heart attack. However, my beloved patted my stomach and laid her head on my shoulder. That helped me calm down enough to remember the speech I had prepared.

"Irene, we must put an end to silence. Banish it forever. I'm sure, for example, that you have engaged in a frenzy of sexual activity with all kinds of mixed-race and black men, American adventurers and revolutionary Sandinistas. Good. Well, you can tell me all about it without any fear. I no longer want us to hide what we do from one another."

Irene gave another laugh. I wondered what it was she found so amusing.

"You're the one who hides things," she, too, said in a playful voice. "I don't hide anything from you. All that happens is I refuse to tell you."

Managua appeared before us in the form of a treeless avenue. The parked cars looked like they belonged in a scrap yard. I must have looked horrified, because Irene drew closer to me and gave me a peck on the cheek.

"You did the right thing coming here," she said. "It's a wonderful country and I already have *lots* of friends."

I looked at her, unable to conceal a touch of indignation at the prospect of a fresh avalanche of extras. I was tempted to say I'd forgotten the spaghetti, but I didn't want to use a pet phrase that belonged to the past. We would need to invent new references there, more tropical ones. Olga had advised me to start anew.

"It all sounds fine to me, Irene. I'll follow you wherever you go."

And I added, discovering the pleasures of boldness:

"After so many minor earthquakes a real one is not going to frighten me."

As we drove to the city in a battered pick-up truck, I thought I wasn't mistaken placing my trust in Irene. It didn't really matter that she had no drivers' license. Everything there seemed to be sustained by a sort of stubborn fatalism born of living side by side with natural disasters. The same things happened there as everywhere else, only more openly. The earth might start roaring at any moment. With any luck, I would be forced to confront an even louder noise, something that would allow me to live without feeling small.

Irene, at the wheel, gave me a sidelong glance, fearful perhaps that I might want to take her away from there. I wondered if she was still the same woman, and if I had ever known who that woman was. I had a sudden need to show her how close I felt to her. I placed my arm around her shoulders and kissed her neck. A shiver ran down her spine. I thought that, even if everything went against us, nothing would deny me the pleasure of continuing to love that intimate stranger. The fact was, I had started to feel at home in the Caribbean, a place I was convinced didn't really exist—like myself, like my distant Caltanissetta, like Saint John of Nepomuk and even my beloved, melancholy Irene. In short, like silence itself.

At that moment I had a wretched idea.

"I've been thinking about something all this time," I lied. "We should write a book about danger."

As if I had just been whipped on the lips, I had the feeling of having kissed the blade of a knife with reckless haste. But then, very slowly, Irene's lips broke into a smile. Although I can't be sure, I believe we both felt for a moment that we had come close to the true subject of that other book which, perhaps, one day, we would end up writing. And that was when a shadow suddenly blocked our view. We heard a loud bang right in front of our faces, followed by the frantic flapping of dying wings as the crumpled body of a huge bird slid down the windshield.

ABOUT THE AUTHOR

PEDRO ZARRALUKI has published, among other novels, *El responsable de las ranas* (1990), winner of the Ciudad de Barcelona and RNE Ojo Crítico awards; *La historia del silencio*, which scooped the Herralde Award (Anagrama, 1994); *Un encargo difícil*, the 2005 Nadal Award-winner and shortlisted for the Fundación José Manuel Lara Award; and *Todo eso que tanto nos gusta* (2008), all of which have been translated into several languages. As well as contributing occasionally to anthologies, he has penned the short story collections *Galería de enormidades* (1989), *Retrato de familia con catástrofe* (1989), and *Humor pródigo* (2007), a collection of comic pieces. His latest collection to hit the shelves is *Te espero dentro* (Destino, February 2013) confirming his place as a master short story teller.

ABOUT THE TRANSLATORS

NICK CAISTOR is an English translator of fiction from Spanish, French, and Portuguese. He worked for many years as a BBC Latin American analyst, and has translated more than thirty-five books from Latin America and Spain, including authors such as Juan Carlos Onetti, Alan Pauls, Andrés Neuman, and Eduardo Mendoza, Juan Marsé and Manuel Vazquez Montalbán. He has twice been awarded the Valle-Inclán prize for translations from Spanish.

LORENZA GARCIA was born and brought up in England, where she graduated from Goldsmith's College, London, with First Class Honours in Spanish and Latin American Studies. Since 2007 she has translated eighteen novels and works of non-fiction from the French and Spanish, most recently in collaboration with Nick Caistor. Their co-translation of Andrés Neuman's novel, *Traveller of the Century* was long-listed in 2013 for the Best Translated Book Award in the USA, and came a close second at the Independent Foreign Fiction Prize 2013. In 2014 the same novel in English was voted runner up for the Valle-Inclán Spanish Translation Prize, as well as being short-listed for the Dublin IMPAC Award.

Lightning Source UK Ltd.
Milton Keynes UK
UKOW02f2051080615

253102UK00001B/5/P

9 788494 283062